Frightfully Cosy and Mild Stories for Nervous Types

Frightfully Cosy and Mild Stories for Nervous Types

By Johnny Mains

To Nicky

Thank you so very much!

love Johnny

Shadow Publishing

Frightfully Cosy and Mild Stories for Nervous Types

This edition © 2012 by Johnny Mains
Cover artwork © 2012 by Richard Sampson

The Song of the Syrinx and Other Callings © 2012 by Stephen Volk
Aldeburgh © 2012. Originally published in *Terror Tales of East Anglia*
Mrs. Claus and the Immaculate Conception © 2012
Cure © 2012
The Tip Run © 2012
Head Soup © 2009. Originally published in *The Aklonomicon*
Dead Forest Air © 2012
The Rookery © 2011. A different version of this story originally
appeared in *Bite Sized Horror*
Prim Suspect © 2012
The Jacket © 2011. Originally published in *Alt-Dead 1*
'I Wish' © 2011. Originally published in *13* (audiobook)
George V © 2011. Originally published in *Voices from the Past*
The Were-Dwarf © 2012
Author's Mumbles © 2012

ISBN: 978-0-9539032-5-2

Shadow Publishing, 194 Station Road, Kings Heath,
Birmingham, B14 7TE, UK
david.sutton986@btinternet.com
http://www.shadowpublishing.webeasysite.co.uk

This book is dedicated to Marnie

Acknowledgements

A massive thanks to David Sutton for seeing the early potential in the collection, then patiently waited for me to deliver the last three, increasingly bizarre stories. Richard Sampson, a friend of long standing and I am utterly thrilled that he agreed to do the cover, Stephen Volk for his great introduction and encouragement, Robert Shearman, Robin Ince for being supportive at every turn, Kirsten Bakis, Terry Oakes and Nicola Budd. Roger Clarke and Simon Su for putting me up and putting up with me every time I drunkenly land in London. Cathy Hurren who is one of the all time greats. Peter Mark May, Anne Billson, Charlie Higson and Marcus Hearn. A collective thanks to Reggie Oliver, Ramsey Campbell and Richard Dalby for their input on the James story. Simon Marshall Jones, Jon Dixon, David Izzat for filming one of the short stories contained in this collection, David Howe and Sam Stone, Alex Miles, David A Riley, John L and Kate Probert, The Vault of Evil, Justin Marriot, Stephen Jones, Val and Les Edwards, Ed and Jean Burke and the late John Burke who I hope would have loved 'Prim Suspect'.

Thanks most of all to my family starting with my wife Lou. At the time of writing this collection we were expecting our first child and now as you are reading this book, I am hallucinating through lack of sleep and posting thousands of baby pictures on Facebook. Our child Marnie is amazing, Lou has been amazing through the stitching together of this book and I think a shout-out should go to all writer's spouses. They put up with a lot!

I would also like to thank my extended family who consist of Bob, Matty, Shozza, Ben and Tom who really make me feel like one of their own. And last but not least, Biscuit, the best dog in the world.

Johnny Mains

Contents

FOREWORD

This collection was originally going to be 'The Difficult Second Collection' but then I discovered that the 'popular disc jockey' Chris Moyles called his latest 'bestseller' 'The Difficult Second Book' and that put paid to that.

The title for this book comes in part from a reviewer who called my first collection 'awfully cosy and mild'. The sentence tickled me so much so (though I didn't agree with the review!) that I thought I'd pinch it and make it near unrecognisable for this new collection.

Johnny Mains,
Devon

THE SONG OF THE SYRINX,
AND OTHER CALLINGS
AN INTRO TO JOHNNY MAINS'
'DIFFICULT SECOND COLLECTION'

By Stephen Volk

I WROTE MY FIRST horror book when I was fifteen years old. It took that long, frankly, only because it wasn't until my fifteenth birthday that I was given a Brother portable typewriter by my grandmother, and that made the production of the book a whole lot easier, because my handwriting was marginally less decipherable than the meanderings of a drunken spider who'd crawled from an ink well.

Production? Yes. Because, you see, I was publishing it too. Oh yes. In fact, most of the effort went into painting the cover, on the kind of shiny white cardboard you used to get when you bought a shirt. At least as much effort went into the artwork—some zombified or blood-dripping ne'er-do-well—as went into the actual stories, each of which took up no more than one page of typescript. The budding author bought a ring binder from John Menzies in town. He bought a hole punch (not a massive call for hole punches in those days). I must've done twenty, thirty stories. *That's a book isn't it? Thirty pages?* It was to me, then.

The truth is, they were hopelessly derivative, and I was hopelessly in love. Derivative to the extent they were mostly very poor imitations of stories I'd read in the likes of the *Pan Books of Horror Stories*. And 'in love' to the extent that those books in the mid-to-late sixties and others like them had started to excite me like no other books I'd read before.

This, I now find, I share with many horror writers of my acquaintance.

3

They know that the *Seventh Pan Book* had that skeleton-silhouette on the cover that gave us all nightmares, and the *Fifth Pan* cover had that terribly sixties woman with a Jackie Kennedy haircut and half her head a skull.

The former is where I first read 'The Fur Brooch' by Dulcie Gray, and 'The Monkey's Paw' by W. W. Jacobs. In the latter, as I now thumb through its dry and brown-edged pages, I see I've margin-marked in the contents the stories 'Claire de Lune' by Seabury Quinn, 'Lukundoo' by Edward Lucas White, 'Men Without Bones' by Gerald Kersh, and 'Hand in Hand' by M. S. Waddell. So they must've had some special impression. And I'm absolutely convinced they had a formative impression on my becoming a writer and the kind of writing I— we—set out to do.

Johnny Mains is one of this happy clan of *Pan*-theists, if you will.

I do not have to fight to persuade him of my interest in their cultural influence or impact. As with my other fellow travellers, he simply 'gets it' and our shared enthusiasm for them goes un-debated.

In fact, he has gone further than me, in that he's not only been a fan but a champion of these lost masterpieces of the macabre. His assembling of a reunion of the old authors of the Pan anthologies at the World Horror Con in Brighton, was one of the supreme highlights of any Con I've been to. And Johnny's delight on the day was palpable, and infectious.

From the collection you are about to read, I am sure he shares a lot of my other memories and acquisitions. The Arrow Dennis Wheatley's and Bram Stokers with their distinctive yellow spines. The Panther Lovecraft anthologies of the same era. John Burke's masterly and unforgettable novelisation of *Dr Terror's House of Horrors*. Perhaps even John Garforth's *Avengers* tie-ins, or (long shot, this) *The Coffin Things* by Michael Avallone.

These tomes, alongside Ballard, Hammer, Wyndham, and Kneale, were our grotesque and uncanny touchstones. More important, ultimately, than any exams or work experience placements. They were tales we took into adulthood as prized possessions. No stretch to say, they became who we were. And many of us have felt the urge to repay that debt. With stories that both pay homage to an enormous influence (in my case encompassing *Journey to the Unknown*, *The Stone Tape*, and other TV and film fare), but also adding something of our own.

Johnny's stories collected herein are happily free of obvious pastiche, which is good. Personally I prefer my terror tales told with a straight face, and even the bleakest humour is the better for that. Yes, there is the smile of nostalgia to know the tradition from whence they came, but they are subversive in their sharp observation and accumulation of detail which elevates them far above the parodic or tongue-in-cheek.

'The Tip Run' turns on a single, nightmarish, image, whereas 'The Rookery' is all the more gut-wrenching for its autobiographical veracity. 'Cure' is horribly succinct: an appalling, simple idea, well told. 'I Wish' nods openly to 'The Monkey's Paw', whilst 'Head Soup' (perhaps my favourite) imagines the horrid truth behind a horror writer's powers of imagination, or otherwise. 'Dead Forest Air' boldly takes an unspeakable subject and renders it freshly terrifying, with the bitter tang of authenticity adding to the sense of foreboding, and 'Aldeburgh' stalks and twists around a master of the macabre like a literary trap waiting to be sprung.

These stories absorbed and disturbed me. And confirmed to me that Johnny Mains not only carries a flame for the old horrors, but wants to cause a bit of a conflagration of his own.

The most fitting result would be if the next generation of horror readers will look back with pleasure and affection at *his* tales, as we did with the *Pans* and *Fontanas* of our ill-begotten youth.

A little scared. A little troubled. But enormously grateful.
I think they will.
I think *you* will....

Stephen Volk
www.stephenvolk.net

ALDEBURGH

H E HAD TRIED IN VAIN to communicate with the Provost, but his letters remained unanswered, much to his frustration. Joseph took up lodgings in Dedworth Road and waited for the Eton "half" to end and for the Provost to be at leisure. He had the money to wait, and could, if need be, stay until the end of the decade. He spent his time either 'loitering' around Eton or frequenting the Five Bells on Sheet Street. He thought he had become a very effective shadow, but it was all to no avail: the Provost had either been alarmed by his correspondence or was just someone who loathed to go out of doors. Joseph thought that it might be a mixture of the two.

The day after the college broke for Long Leave he spotted him, in the school yard emerging from under the arch of Lupton's Tower, walking hurriedly, perhaps towards the school library; three heavy-looking tomes under his left arm. He looked elderly but he was still a big, sprightly man and appeared to relish in taking his time.

As Joseph approached him, the Provost smiled cautiously, and seeing that the younger man at least *looked* like a gentleman, bade him good day.

'Doctor Montague Rhodes James?' said Joseph, stopping in front of him. James' smile faded, his eyes betrayed a faint recognition, then became quizzical, almost wary.

'Yes?'

'My name is Joseph Payton, and I believe that you wrote about my father Percival in your story 'A Warning to the Curious.' I beg of you, please tell me what you know.' He stared at James hard, the older man's face crumpled somewhat; he looked like he needed to sit down.

'I'm sorry, I have no idea of what you refer to. It was a fictional story,' he mumbled, fending him away with his free arm. Joseph tried to reach out to make him stay but James pushed his shoulder with surprising power. 'You will leave me be, unless you would like for me to call on the porter?'

'Sir, call on the porter as much as you like. Perhaps he won't be as dismissive of my belief that *you* killed my father!'

They were harsh words to say, but they had the desired effect.

The Provost's eyes narrowed. 'Where are you staying, young man?'

'I have lodgings with Mrs Humphries on Dedworth, they cater for a better class of client,' Joseph said, breathing in deeply and puffing out his chest. James appeared not to notice this display.

'Very well. I shall call on you tomorrow. Have your landlady prepare an early breakfast.'

'You will call?'

'Yes.' Dr James walked off, his black gown billowing about him, leaving Joseph standing there, following the old man's journey until he was out of sight.

'I think we should start at the end,' Joseph began, unfolding his newspaper and revealing the hardback which bore the name of the offending story. He opened the book where he had placed his marker, coughed, and started to read.

'*You don't need to be told that he was dead. His tracks showed that he had run along the side of the battery, had turned sharp round the corner of it, and, small doubt of it, must have dashed straight into the open arms of someone who was waiting there. His mouth was full of sand and stones, and his teeth and jaws were broken into bits. I only glanced once at his face.*'

Joseph had tears in his eyes. He blinked and one solitary trail of saltwater ran down the side of his face.

He shut the book carefully on his forefinger so as to not lose his place and began to speak. 'When I was ten, my mother sat me down, patted my knee and told me quite calmly that my father had been found dead on a beach in Aldeburgh. He died a savage and lonely death, but this I didn't find out until I was sixteen. I had asked the question of what happened to him. My mother gave me these clippings from the *East Anglian Times*, dated 1923.' He passed over two small newspaper cuttings. The passage of twelve years had made the cheap paper brown and brittle.

TREASURE-HUNTER FOUND DEAD IN ALDEBURGH
The body of Percival Payton, from Hunstanton, was found Thursday, April 25th...

James handed back the first and glanced at the headline of the second. It was dated June 1923.

VERDICT OF WILFUL MURDER BY PERSON OR PERSONS UNKNOWN IN STRANGE CASE OF TREASURE-SEEKER

Joseph continued, 'As you well know, your book containing the story was published in 1925. I would never have become suspicious of you, sir, had I not been given a copy of your book as a gift last year. The shock I received on reading the story was horrific. There, laid bare, the 'facts'. You were staying in the area during April, when a man was found dead on the beach. 'And... th... though it's a slight description,' he started to stammer as he became more agitated, 'when you say...' Joseph opened up the book again, and skipped back through the story erratically until he came to the correct page. '*He was rather a rabbity anæmic subject—light hair and light eyes—but not unpleasing,*' you describe him to a tee. He was a "treasure-hunter" as the papers put it, and from what my mother told me, a pretty poor one—a few shards of Roman pottery and maybe the odd coin were the entire fruit of his labours. But he was enthusiastic about his pastime and a true lover of the countryside.' He was rambling now. 'He took many photographs—the camera and eight or nine plates were returned along with his body.' The old man's eyes never left Joseph's. Joseph seemed to notice for the first time and breathed deeply. Then more quietly, 'I have the photographs of a church and of a coat of arms that contains the three crowns of East Anglia. It was indeed in the porch of the church.' From the back of the book he removed a heavy grain, cream envelope and opening it up slowly, took out several photographs, some of which he laid out on the table in front of James. Indeed there was the church, also a picture of two kindly-looking old men, one of them was the Rector, the other, presumably, the sexton.

'So,' continued Joseph, much quieter now 'the evidence is as follows: you were in the area at the same time as my father, you have ably described his looks and his occupation and you have also written that he had taken photographs of a church and had seen a coat of arms with three crowns on it. My father's name and the name you use in the book is only a single letter removed! You said yesterday that it was a work of fiction, but I must ask again sir, what do you know of my father?'

Joseph had kept hold of two more photographs and he placed them gently and deliberately on top of the others. Dr. James looked at them for a long while. He saw himself, from a distance, in which he appeared to be studying the newspaper intently in the reading room at the White Lion Hotel, the other, talking at the front of the hotel to two ladies one of whom appeared to be handing him something. James thought it might have been a book, one of his own that he had been asked to sign.

'My father took these photographs, they are clearly of you. Tell me, what do you know?'

The silence was broken by Mrs. Humphries who entered the

parlour with a fresh tray of tea. James nodded tiredly at her: his rest the night before had been non-existent. Joseph nodded his thanks after she poured, and as she left, reached inside his jacket and pulled out one final photograph. It was his father, Percival Payton, a candid shot, taken several years before his death, sitting in the garden, a young Joseph on his knee.

Dr James reached down to his leather satchel, placed it on his knees and opened it deliberately, the metal buckles clanging as he undid the straps and folded the top back. He rummaged around and pulled out a rather substantial sheaf of papers, covered with his almost unintelligible handwriting.

'These are the notes I made when writing "A Warning to the Curious",' he glanced at Joseph over the rim of his glasses. His tone was sincere, but weary. 'It was written on my return to Eton of course, but the sad death of your father was the catalyst for the tale and I am sorry that I used his passing in this way. It is unforgiveable and I am truly contrite, this you must believe.'

The old man knew that this was not enough. He glanced at the notes in his hands. The morning light made the pages glow. He continued.

'I was staying at the White Lion hotel with a good friend and his acquaintance; they would spend most of their time on the golf course and I, invariably, would spend my time walking long distances or sitting on the shorefront reading, according to my wont, detective fiction or 'thrillers', as I believe they are now called. In the evening we would meet for supper then retire to the reading room for brandy and a little conversation. It was here that I first met your father, and the tale is entirely correct at this point; he came in looking rather distracted, asked if he could make company with us, and after a while I engaged him with some small talk. He told me that he was an antiquarian and a collector of curios and naturally I asked him what it was in the area he was looking for. It was then he told me the story of his meeting the reverend and the three crowns of Anglia, about which I hasten to add, I already knew of. He also mentioned a family as the protectors of the site of the last remaining crown. They had done so for many, many years and the last in their line had passed away not long before, maybe only thirty years or so. It was your father's intention to find this crown, dig it up and make his name, because from his appearance it did not seem, if I may be vulgar, that he was a man of means.

'All in the room were curious at this point, and we talked about the legality of any discovery...'

'Were the family who protected the crown called Ager?' Joseph interrupted.

The Provost smiled briefly, thought for a second and continued.

'No, they were not. Although I wrote about something based on a true event, as a writer of fiction I knew the story would never be believed as true. Legend is legend, and the crowns and their protectors are purely such. But should that stop someone from believing that they exist? And of course I was not the first to document the crown's existence; they are a pertinent, if obscure legend. I must say though that whilst writing my tales I do not like to make things easy should a reader decide to take up the mantle and do a little... research.

'We talked about the legality of his discovery and we all agreed that he would receive a substantial sum from the crown if no claim was made by land owners. He believed the current land owner to be without relations, so would have seen the lion's share of any wealth.

'At the end of the evening we parted company, having agreed it the find of a lifetime should he succeed and we wished him luck. We did not ask to be involved in the hunt, although it *was* extremely interesting.'

'When was the next time you saw him?' Joseph asked, taking James' proffered papers and slowly leafing through them.

'The next time I saw him he was dead on the beach.'

Joseph looked up, startled, the colour drained from his face.

'But the story says...'

'Fool!' Dr. James' anger was up. His neck was beginning to mottle, the colour crept slowly up to his chin. He breathed in deeply and closed his eyes. The anger dissipated in slow receding waves, when he opened his eyes again he saw that Joseph was staring at him with fury in *his* eyes.

'We were in the reading room, when one of the waiters came in to tell us that the gentleman we had been talking to a day previously was believed to be dead,' James continued slowly. 'We were shocked, horribly so, and we rushed to the scene which was quite some distance away. The night was beginning to draw in, and by the time we got there it was near dark. There were five or six people in attendance, carrying lamps. A doctor had been called and pronounced your father to be dead. We were not asked why we were there and in retrospect it was rather ghoulish of us to go, but with the information that we had, if it appeared that he was murdered, we could have been of some use.'

'Did you attend the inquest?'

'No, we did not, but I will explain why in a moment. Your father was partially covered in sand from head to toe, and his mouth was full of small pebbles. His neck was broken, but I elaborated of course in the story further injuries to attain shock, create an impact. We waited for a policeman to attend; while there was a doctor in town, a policeman had to be raised from another village, and we were with the body for a further hour and a half.

'Once he arrived, of course we were asked about our connection to him and we told the policeman all we knew. He was satisfied with our story, and why wouldn't he be? The remains were removed, and two days later we ventured to Cambridge and in time there was an inquest at which neither myself, my friend or his acquaintance were called to give evidence at. I still have that letter if you wish to look at it. I remember placing a phone call that day and was told that our statements given were enough.' Dr. James sighed, his face puffy and he removed his spectacles and wiped them with a fine cloth.

'I don't know if your father found the crown and had been murdered for it or if they remain the legend that they always were. I sit here in front of you and I can only state, with every fibre of my being, that I was in no way responsible for your father's death and I am truly sorry that I used and indeed blackened his memory in the way I did. While unforgivable, these wild accusations have to stop. I am a writer of supernatural fiction, that is *all*.'

Tears spilled silently down Joseph's face. James softened and reached out with his liver spotted hand and patted the younger man's knee before squeezing it affectionately.

'I lost him when I needed him the most,' Joseph said quietly, looking embarrassed. 'I was very directionless as a teenager, most troubled, and if it wasn't for the dedication of my mother and my father's brother, I would be in a worse-off state than I am now.' Joseph didn't elaborate further.

James reached into his waistcoat pocket and pulled out a slightly battered pocket watch. He flipped it open, and satisfied that not too much of the morning had been eaten up, snapped it closed. He got up, retrieving the manuscript and put it into his bag.

'While I don't deny that you've been through a very trying time, I have stated the facts to the best of my knowledge. It has been a pleasure to make your acquaintance, even though you made a very serious charge against me—but we all make mistakes and say things we don't mean when emotional.'

Joseph looked shocked. 'You mean that's it? That's all you have to say on the matter?'

'Yes,' snapped James, as if his comforting actions of only a few moments ago had never happened. 'I have helped as much as I am able. If you need further assistance, please leave a message with the porter who will pass it on.'

With that, he left the room, bidding Mrs. Humphries a good day on his way out. Joseph picked up the two newspaper clippings and slid them into the envelope along with the photographs of James at Aldeburgh. Then it came to him, the simplest of plans and he smiled, albeit a little sadly. Montague Rhodes James was going to help him find out what happened to his father whether he liked it or not.

The car pulled up outside the hotel he frequented on every visit to Aldeburgh, The White Lion. Getting out, M. R. James breathed in deeply, the salt in the air making his nostrils tingle, and not unpleasantly. He waited as the driver retrieved his luggage from the boot of the car and then proceeded to walk into the hotel, Dr. James following behind leisurely.

He had been in two minds whether to come to Aldeburgh; of course he had returned every year since the death on the beach, but it was Joseph's appearance that had rattled him so. He was aware of the letters that he'd initially been sent by the younger man and had read them, hoping that if he simply ignored them the nuisance would go away. It was extremely foolish of him to dress a real life story with supernatural overtones, never thinking for a second that anyone would put two and two together and *definitely* not the son of the deceased. What he had desperately wanted to say, but daren't, as Joseph would have been mortified, was that the stories he wrote, in the main, were merely whimsies, written while slightly drunk on good brandy and primarily for his colleagues, or, more recently, a select gathering of Eton whom he enjoyed transfixing with what he liked to call "a pleasing terror". He was pleased with the external interest in his work and his collections were very fine, but the fact of the matter was that it wouldn't bother him in the slightest if the public stopped buying his books.

In the end Aldeburgh's charms were too great to resist, they always had been. He thought back to the first time he visited and little had changed in the village since then. Ironically enough he had struggled with the notion of writing about Aldeburgh in a short story in the first place, thinking that if he revealed its locations the magic would be lost. So he changed the name and mixed up the ingredients slightly, but for the discerning armchair detective it wouldn't take a lot to figure what little seaside village on the Suffolk coast he was talking about.

As James was taken to his room, the receptionist told him that his friend, who would be joining him on this trip, was delayed by several days due to an aunt dying suddenly. Thinking that he would do well to whittle away a few hours after he unpacked, he went back downstairs and looked through the various books that were on offer in the reading room. The only thing that held any interest was a copy of *New Tales of Horror By Eminent Authors*—a book that James had in his library, but was yet to read. He looked through the contents and his nose wrinkled when he saw Arthur Machen's name, but Richard Middleton and M. P. Shiel would soon make up for Machen's inclusion.

He took the book outside with him, the wind had picked up ever so slightly, making him glad that he had put on his jacket. It wasn't too oppressive weather to read though, so James ambled across the road to the beach and hired a deckchair. Once he had found a suitably level spot, he began to read.

Several of the stories were utter tripe and obviously written by hacks who had no understanding of the finer points of the English language, but James gruffly conceded that the anthology did have a vague synchronicity to it, the stories ebbed and flowed evenly.

Loath as he was to admit it, several of the stories had him completely enthralled, so much so that he didn't notice the presence standing next to him.

'Good day to you,' the presence said.

He looked up, dismayed, recognising the voice instantly. It was

Joseph.

'What are you doing here?' James barked. 'Trying to ruin my holiday?'

'No sir,' Joseph almost sneered, 'trying to find the person who *killed* my father.' He was holding a deck chair and proceeded to open it up. Dr. James made no move to get up and leave.

'The truth, sir, is that I didn't know that you were going to be here, but I made an educated guess and hoped that you would be. It's fine, I'm not staying at the hotel, I would never be that impudent, I'll room at another place in town.' Joseph sat down and made himself comfortable, putting his hands deep into the pockets of his long trench coat. He looked at the Provost steadily. James sighed, closed the book and placed it on his knee.

'So what do you plan to do whilst here? Apart from the obvious, of course. And where's your luggage?' James said, and was surprised at the acidity in his voice.

'I travel light. Clothes can be washed and dried before bed and before I rise. But if you really want to know what I'll do here is that I'm going make enquiries to try and discover where the 'Ager' homestead was, then go there and look for signs of disturbance in the earth and then take it from there. I'll try and get under the skin of whoever killed my father, my presence will hopefully shock his killer to try and come after me...'

'And what will you do if he or she does?'

'I'll shoot them where they stand.' From his right pocket, the one furthest away from James, Joseph pulled out a Webley revolver. He didn't appear to be concerned by the look of shock that appeared on James' face.

'And what happens if you make a mistake and you shoot the wrong person? You'll swing, mark my words. And I wouldn't lift a finger, not if you gunned somebody down in cold blood.' James let the book drop from his knee onto the sand.

'And if I shot you? There would be circumstantial evidence in my favour.'

'Are you insane, man?' Dr James leapt up out of his chair and for the first time in a long time, a searing bolt of pain ran down his leg, the result of an accident many years before. He gasped, clutching at it, sitting back down, looking at Joseph furiously.

'If I haven't persuaded you of my innocence, then I am clearly talking to someone who has taken leave of his senses.'

'He could have found the crown, and you being such an *antiquarian* could have killed him and stolen it from him. You're elderly and jaded now, granted, but go back to then, I think you could have overpowered him. He was after all a 'rabbity anæmic subject.' Joseph spat the sentence out, such was the bitterness in it.

Dr James guffawed.

'Oh, my dear boy.' He lifted his glasses up slightly and wiped a solitary laughter tear away from his wrinkled skin. 'After your father died, I made one or two enquiries myself and discovered approximately what I believe to be the location of the "Ager" place. If you want, we can walk there and you can go forage to your heart's content. If you find something and it's the *mythical* crown then you can show that I am nothing but a foolish scholar whose love of fantastical stories has clearly gone to his head. But I will say this for the last time. I am an author of ghost and supernatural fiction who was inspired by the story your father told me and then inspired by his death, as uncaring as that sounds, to write a work of fiction which was part-based on true events. I cannot apologise enough. But after I show you the "Ager" place, I expect you to leave me alone. No more threats or posturing from you, please. Stay in the village if you wish or go back to your own home but you will no longer intrude on my privacy. I will summon the police and you can tell them all the stories under the sun.' Dr. James got up again, this time more slowly. He favoured his leg and his face relaxed when there was no pain.

'We can walk along the beach for a while before we walk out of the village and go in-country for a few miles. It's a long walk, made longer by the way that we'll go, but I thought you might like to stop for a moment where they found your father.' The words hung on the air, waiting for Joseph to snatch at them. He was up in an instant, the gun back in his pocket.

'Come on then Provost, we've walking to do.'

The wind had eased somewhat and half a mile further down the beach, James realised that he had left the horror book behind. He hoped that it wouldn't get taken by the tide; he hated doing disservices to books, no matter their content. His leg was fine, it wasn't giving him any trouble as yet, even though they were walking on small pebbles, but he thought that by the time he reached the "Ager" site, it might cause him considerable discomfort.

Twenty minutes later and James stopped abruptly, looking intently at the Martello tower and where the cut in the middle of the dunes were.

'It was here. This is where he was found. I'll leave you with your thoughts for a while.'

Joseph's answer surprised him.

'No.'

They continued to walk in silence, the wind became stronger, one sudden gust nearly caught Joseph unawares who was slender and had almost no meat to his bones.

They left the beach and soon walked down a high-hedged lane, the wind here was dampened somewhat. Twisting and turning their way through the countryside, Dr. James pointed in the direction of a small copse of woods on the top of a slight mound about half a mile away.

'It's just beyond those trees. You'll be able to see why when we get there, there's a gap in them that lets you see the beach and sea beyond for miles in either direction,' Dr. James explained.

And then they arrived; a three-quarters ruined cottage, the roof of which had collapsed, taking most of the house with it. Thick brambles grew everywhere and seemed to protect the cottage from would-be intruders. The trees surrounding them swayed in the strong breeze. James sat on a wind-blown tree trunk about ten metres away as Joseph reached into his pocket and pulled out his envelope and from it, two photographs. He stared at them, then held them out at arm's length, and moved around in a circle till he thought he had come to the place the first photograph depicted. The wind tried its best to whip the photograph's from the young man's hand, but he quickly put them back in the envelope and into an inside pocket of his trench coat.

'This is the place,' Joseph said, with a grin on his face. 'You can go now, Provost.'

James looked up at the younger man. The grin had vanished, and was replaced by a cold certainty. James had expected him to be holding the gun.

'Very well. I hope you find what you're looking for. If you do however, I have no wish to see it, so don't come gloating.' James got up from his seat and walked away down the gentle slope, his left foot coming down on the corpse of a small sparrow and he winced as the bones crunched under his weight.

James was adamant that nothing was going to spoil the rest of his holiday and he even hoped that the book he had left behind on the shingle wasn't too spoiled, or had had pages torn from it. The wind was certainly picking up again, stronger than before, nearly pushing the Provost over on a few occasions.

Of course, Joseph would come back empty-handed and James wondered how long it would be before the accusations began. And then there was the gun. The Provost decided that as soon as he got into the village he would call on the policeman and say that there was a rather unstable chap who was a danger to himself and to others. Even if there were questions to be asked, James knew he could answer them, even if the situation was odd and might raise eyebrows. But in his favour was the esteem and probity his name carried; he would be believed, there would be no reason why he shouldn't be.

Passing the Martello tower and continuing down the lonely stretch of sand, something whipped passed James, carried with the strong wind. He stopped and cocked his ear. It was high pitched, disjointed and nearly vanished under the increasing roar of the wind but it was almost as if James was *meant* to hear it.

'I put it back! I put it back!'

Dr James turned around. In the distance he could see Joseph sprinting towards him and he was running very, very fast, no doubt being helped along by the severe gusts that would see several trees felled before the day was out. This far away Joseph's face was an undistinguishable blob of white.

The wind blew into James' face and again, that same phrase, now sounding like a scream, was as loud as if it had been shouted in his ear.

'I put it back... OH GOD!'

The sky, which was aphotic and angry before, suddenly turned an inky black, though at eye level there was still enough light to see; James' vision had become grainy and scratched.

Joseph was carried off his feet, along the beach, about a metre into the air. He went no further up, but it appeared as if he was levitating. James looked on in horror as suddenly the younger man's body was folded back on itself, the heels of his shoes slamming into his head, spine snapping as easily as a dead twig. It sounded like a starting pistol.

Then the wind dropped, jarring James with its suddenness. Joseph fell to the ground.

Dr James began running as fast as his old body would take him, his leg screaming with pain, his heart trip-hammering in his chest, a bird fluttering its wings against its cage, trying to get out. The sky slowly reverted back to being grey and overcast.

When he reached Joseph, it was plain to see that he was quite dead. His neck was broken; head twisted around so much so his face was buried in the sand. His arms and legs were in positions unfathomable to the human eye. Bones poked out of fabric.

'Oh Joseph,' James croaked, sure that the violence was going to re-visit any second. 'I didn't know that...' He couldn't think of the right words to say, and to dwell further on it... therein lay the madness which was only a whisper away from taking him. But whatever had been here wouldn't return unless whatever it was that Joseph had found at the "Ager" place was disturbed again. Of which the Provost clearly had no intention of ever doing.

His hands shaking violently, Dr James opened up the dead man's jacket and felt for the envelope which he eased out and slipped into his own. When Joseph was found, James didn't want anyone to look at the photographs and go foraging. It wasn't lost on James that if he had found the crown when he had visited the "Ager" place, he would have met his end as violently as Joseph had.

He slowly limped away from the broken remains, an old man confused and shaken by the invisible line between his writing and the truly unknown. All the way back to the hotel he felt as if he was being watched by an unseen presence witnessing his every move, knowing that the executor of the carnage that had been wrought upon poor Joseph Payton was the force that was bound with the last remaining crown of East Anglia.

Knowing that he shouldn't, but feeling as if he *must*, he turned around to look back one last time and standing over the body was a man in what had once been a respectable suit but was now almost rags. He was thin, 'rabbity looking', as Dr. James might have said, and his dark, broken mouth was hanging open in an almost soundless scream of hopeless grief. James turned from this and, despite his leg, now excruciatingly painful, began to run desperately over the shingle.

Arriving back at the hotel, James immediately retired to bed, and when his friend arrived, several days later, Dr. James simply spent most of his time in the empty reading room, drinking brandy and waiting for the holiday to be over, truly expecting that at any moment Joseph would be found and the link between James, the boy and the boy's father would be unearthed.

Once back at Eton, Montague Rhodes James decided that the trip to Aldeburgh was to be his last. Joseph's broken body and his father standing next to him haunted Dr James until he died, a year later.

MRS. CLAUS AND THE
IMMACULATE CONCEPTION

Dedicated to Rob Shearman

SOMETIME IN THE FUTURE...

M RS. CLAUS GOT OUT OF BED and padded across the
sealskin rug to the neatly kept dresser. She sat down in
front of it and looked at herself in the mirror.

Not bad for a near 900 year old, she thought to herself as she wiped
off the remnants of last night's face mask with a luxuriant polar
bear fat emollient. Apart from the crow lines around the eyes—
because she was always so *jolly*, and the tell-tale wrinkling of
smokers lips—she looked nothing like she did on the rare number
of Christmas cards with her "likeness" that she archived dutifully,
year upon year. A plump, jolly (there's that word again) old duck
who looked to be in her early seventies, tending to Santa's beard
with an elaborately carved wooden comb was not who she was.
She was tall, broad and built like a killing machine.

She wiped the last of the thick green paste away and stood up,
walked towards the wardrobe and pulled on her red skirt and
white cardigan that depicted, through the wonders of seventies
knitting patterns, a reindeer flying a Sopwith Camel.

Dressed, she got her cigarettes from her bedside table and lit
one, relishing the bite of the smoke deep in her lungs.

'Santa! Have you risen from your slumber?' she shouted.

Silence.

She left the room and knocked on the great oak door. Receiving
no answer she turned the jade door knob briefly to the left and
pushed, the hinges creaking with the same sound as a tree toppling over.

The room was bare, apart from a bed in the middle and a photo-graph of Santa before he became Santa. He used to be Mike Marshall, once a security guard from Effingham on the Stour. In the photograph he was standing next to an elderly woman and he had a worried look on his face. Now the man, once known for his love of collecting Victorian medical books, looked worried no longer. He was dead.

Santa's face, what you could see through the beard, was tinged blue. There was a crumb of bread hanging off the bottom lip. Mrs. Claus bent over and brushed it away. It disappeared into the beard.

'You poor thing, you were a good Santa,' she whispered. Mrs. Claus left, closing the door gently behind her and went to a bank of buttons at the top of the stairs. She pressed the bottom right hand side button, fresher looking than the rest. A mournful klaxon reverberated throughout the building. In the workshops, the helpers began to cry.

The man lying upstairs was the sixth Santa Mrs. Claus had looked after. They normally lasted fifty years before keeling over. Once a Santa had passed away, the hunt to find a suitable replace-ment would begin immediately.

Christmas was too important ever to be cancelled. The sanity of the world depended on it.

The helpers tended to Mike's body, which had now shrunk back to something that was a little thinner, not as morbidly obese. It *did* seem unfair that every new Santa was expected to eat until they hit fighting weight, all that extra pressure on the heart, making death more of a certainty than an alluded ambiguity, a far away, little dreamed of finality. It was true that Mike had been a 105 year old man—the spirit of Christmas and a little teaspoon of serum after tea, plus the length of tenure had stretched out his life which would have ended at seventy, given local and cultural variations.

His beard was cropped close, then shaved off completely, the beard hair was then thrown in the fire. Mike was dressed in a finely tailored black suit by Mrs. Claus; it was slit up the back—as the body would expand as decomposition would bloat and transmogrify. Mrs. Claus led out the funeral cortege, every helper lined the walkway from the main house, all the way past the reindeer who were brought out from the stables, their inky black eyes glistened in the afternoon sun, to a small cemetery which bore four beautifully carved headstones and a plain one. Each one apart from Santa Three had SANTA, HE HELPED CHILDREN ALL OVER THE WORLD. HE WILL BE DEEPLY MISSED. The third Santa's inscription was blank.

The ramifications of the Santa Three had nearly brought the whole operation down. He had taken his love of children a little *too* far. Once he had arrived back home at the nth Pole, Mrs. Claus took him round the back and slit his throat with the knife she used for slaughtering. Edvard Olafsun from Stockholm, a predatory paedophile who had somehow managed to pull the wool over Santa Claus Inc. spent his last moments on Earth marvelling at how pretty his blood looked on the snow.

It was therefore decided that all future holders of the name would be chemically castrated. Extra incentives were added to the job description to dull the loss. In all honesty, they were not needed. People who ended up becoming Santa were thankful for escaping the misery and pointlessness of their old lives and that they would be doing some genuine good for the many, instead of being a constant pain in the side to the few.

After Mike was buried, Mrs. Claus invited the helpers upstairs for nibbles and drinks —the only time they were ever allowed up into the main part of the house. As they ate small tartlets of seal cheese and pesto, a snowstorm swept through the bleak valley and covered the new grave.

*

Ignatius Solo looked solemnly at the rather expressive graffiti before shrugging his shoulders and moving on. It was a sad fact that as soon as the council got off of its arse to paint away the xenophobic, sickening bile that was on every wall from the bus station to his house, it would appear again overnight—despite the promises from the corpulent power-hungry suits.

He had the day's red-top under his arm and a bottle of Monster Bite Whisky and two packs of Red Apple Cigarettes in a faded plastic bag-for-life. He slowly made his way through the ravaged estate that was his home, past 54 Rillington Place where Old Man Trevor went a bit mad one night and beat his wife over two hundred times on the head with a ball-pein hammer (there wasn't much left), under the underpass where a group of feral kids (who only had the courage to do it at night) had raped and beaten a fifty year old woman who died in hospital the next day and through the blood-spattered pavements of Brush Street until he arrived at McGarry Towers. The lift had never worked since day two. Ignatius took the stairs slowly and surely, his cigarette habit dictating he'd be out of puff by the second riser. He opened the door to his flat, number 60 and dumped the whisky in the kitchen. Walking through to the small living space, he fired up his aging Acer laptop, the protesting beeps warning him that he needed to plug it in to charge.

His flat was at the top of the tower, it gave him some comfort— the troublemakers never came up that far, they preferred a quick, easy, getaway if the police were ever called. Ignatius plugged in the battery pack and switched on the plug at the wall, the red charge light started winking on and off—the electric heartbeat that died when it was fully charged.

Ignatius checked his phone for missed calls, there were none, and then looked out of the window, down at the street far below. There seemed to be a scrap going on, yep, there definitely was. He got his binoculars from the small table where the laptop was and looked down at the scene. It was over as quickly as it had begun, a young male was suffering from a case of death—there was a lot of blood and a knife sticking out of the side of his head.

Ignatius sighed and went to the telephone and dialled 999. When the operator asked for his name, he hung up. He went and poured himself a generous helping of whisky and drank deeply, wincing slightly as the alcohol bit his insides, set him on fire, perked up his senses. He sat down at the computer and checked his emails, there were none. He was just about to close the browser when an email pinged into his inbox. It was from Santa Inc. and said simply **JOB OPPORTUNITY**. His heart leapt in his chest and sped up like a galloping pit pony. He clicked on the mail, which took its time opening. He cursed NTL for being one of the worst internet providers in the country.

At last it did and the email read thus:

> *To whom it may concern,*
>
> *Yesterday saw the passing of Santa Six, and the search for a new Santa begins. It is no understatement to say that this is the most important job on the planet, and that the happiness of billions of children depends on your timely visiting throughout all of the different time-zones on Christmas Eve. Please attach your C.V. in Word format (.doc or .docx) and head your email with your name only. This is a rather special time for Santa Inc. The first time that the internet has been utilised to look for a Santa this way, and even though I'm sure that quite a few weirdoes will crawl out of the woodwork—we will find the right man for the job. Please read the attached document for the rules and regulations, which I am all*

sure that you are aware of, having watched the changes Santa Inc. has gone through in the past. While one aspect of becoming Santa has been well documented, on the last three occasions it hasn't put anyone off, such are the rewards.

I await your reply,

Mrs. Claus.

There wasn't a person in the world who didn't know about the troubles that had befallen Santa Inc. In the past, indeed it had almost become brand damaging—and the culprit had yet to be found, though most assumed that he had perished while fleeing across the nth Pole.

Ignatius decided that he was the man for the job. He *had* to be the man for the job. If he didn't get it he would throw a chair through the large window and then follow that down. He put together a letter explaining how good a Santa he'd be, and along with his CV, sent it off.

He spent that evening watching the videos. There were thirty of them in all, each sixty minutes long and featured Ignatius, his wife Larama and two children, Miggy-boo and Dave. He sat there in the gloom of the evening, smoking one Red Apple after the other, drinking his way through the whisky with the hope that he'd be unconscious before putting on the second video.

He had been working that night, that Christmas Eve, ten years before, when he was a happy father, happy husband and a content human being, at one with his lot on Earth. He had met his wife Larama on a cruise ship, he was working in the kitchen as a pot washer and she was the hired talent, a Bolivian singer with coffee coloured skin, long black hair that reached down to her behind and a behind that wiggled seductively when she walked. Her eyes twinkled in the glare of the sodium lights and if it had not been for a quirk of fate, the pair would never have met and fallen in love.

The head chef had got drunk one lonely and suicidal night and held a metal barbeque skewer against his eye and ran into the wall, killing himself instantly. That would have been fine, he would have been found and dispatched overboard without any of the guests finding about it, but the rats (and there are always rats, no matter what boat, ship or cruise liner you go on) decided to eat as much of the head chef as they could before he was found, but chef didn't agree with the rats and they ended up having rat shitters all over the boat, which meant that one thousand guests and hired staff were holed up in the ballroom until they could get into the nearest port which was in Jamaica, and was three more days away. A deep clean was required.

That three day journey of hell is another tale and will not be told today (if ever), but needless to say, Ignatius and Larama met, fell in love, and he persuaded her to jump ship when the liner finally made its way into Plymouth three months later. She agreed and quickly fell pregnant. And they were happy, deliriously so. Miggy-boo and Dave were the icing on the cake.

So, he had been at work on Christmas Eve when the call had come in; his best friend Jimbo screaming down the phone at him to get home as quickly as possible. Ignatius left everything and never returned. When he arrived at his home, he found it in flames, a raging inferno, eating everything inside, including his family. He had tried to rush in, uncaring about the fate that would befall him, life just wasn't worth living. He managed to come out with a bag full of home videos and nothing else.

The computer 'pinged' behind him. Ignatius got up slowly, turning off the video of his happy, yelling children and walked to the computer, sitting down on the rickety dining room chair and double clicked on the icon.

> From: santajob@santainc.com
> To: Ig.Solo@btinternet.com
> Subject: Santa Job

Dear Ignatius,

Thank you very much for your interest in the role of Santa Claus, but you will not be considered for the job. There is the possibility that you hate Christmas due to the fact you lost your whole family around the festive season. That makes you a loose cannon and someone not to be trusted.

Regards,

Mrs. Claus.

Anger. Pure, unadulterated, intense, awful, terrible anger swept through Ignatius' body until it focused on such a finite point that he thought that his heart might burst with exertion.

Then the inbox pinged again.

The message was from deathtonth@ntl.com and was headed 'The End is Nth'.

He double clicked on it by accident; he had meant to single click and drag it to the trash.

The message said simply.

Ignatius Solomon,

It's time to kill Christmas. Await further instructions.

Ignatius lit up a cigarette and breathed in the smoke heavily, staring at the screen and wondering what the fuck was going to happen next. Jumping out of the window looked like it needn't be an option. He had an inkling that he may have to pack long johns which was fine; he always bought three new pairs at the beginning of every winter as the weather was always apt to turn extremely parky in his neck of the woods.

Mrs. Claus woke up and ran straight to the toilet to throw up. If she had known then she was pregnant she would have cut out her own uterus with the carving knife and thrown the foetus in the sink. But she put it down to the chicken she had eaten for dinner the night before. The hen *had* looked a bit peaky before she had wrung its neck, she thought, wiping her mouth with the back of her hand before she pushed her heaving frame up and away from the toilet. She looked at the green spew with distaste. Sickness was for weaklings. And she couldn't look out of control when the new Santa was due to arrive later on that day.

She washed her face, and walked out of the bedroom and into the freshly painted room that the new Santa was going to spend the next fifty years in. Still she felt sad, she had liked Mike. He had been the best one of the lot—well, the best one of the *imitators*. The real Santa was incomparable.

Mrs. Claus had decided that the new Santa was going to be Phillip White, sixty, from Norwich. He was an ex-chief of police, who had many, many commendations to his name. He was also a widower; in the Skype call Mrs. Claus had with Phillip before telling him to come up to the nth Pole, she was struck by how professional and dedicated he seemed and had a feeling that he would become utterly dedicated to the most important role in the world. The castration was a non-issue as far as Phillip was concerned (although he didn't say that out loud) having suffered from impotence ever since his wife died at the age of thirty and he was thirty-two.

As soon as the Skype conversation was over, she instructed her UK operative to go to Norwich and collect Phillip and drive him to Heathrow where a private jet would be ready to take him to the nth pole.

At the same time Phillip was flying to become Santa Seven, Ignatius was driving up to Loch Lomond. He had been sent several emails, these ones were all encrypted; he'd had to send them through a total of three different secret servers until he had the location of where he was to go at hand. Once he received the locations and the incentives that were involved he was driving towards the motorway as fast as he could. Even the possibility of being killed in action didn't put him off in the slightest; he was getting back at the occasion that killed his wife and children. And if he died in the process? Well, it just meant that he was going to be seeing them that much sooner.

The location was an old youth hostel, closed down in the recent SYHA carnage cuts. The building was now out of sight and out of mind and would be until the building was finally sold and its future determined.

As Ignatius pulled up in front of the building, he saw a group of seven men standing there, smoking and talking amongst themselves. He got out and was instantly welcomed, offered a cigarette which he took, and as he lit up, a black jeep drove up the long drive, and when it stopped, a large man, over seven foot tall got out. He introduced himself as Tom Davis, and it was apparent that he was the head of this little operation. He had a full beard and a belly of mammoth proportions. Ignatius thought that Tom would have had all the suitable qualities needed to become Santa, so he wondered how and why he had been passed over.

Once it was time, they went into the building, the walls covered with posters of young, adventurous walkers going up into the mountainous terrain. The men filed through what used to be the lounge, no television, then the kitchen and dining room where it turned out their presentation was going to be. The table and chairs had been covered in heavy dust sheets. There was, however, a line of empty chairs in front of a screen projection. The screen projected a simple phrase. 'KillingChristmas.'

Tom went through the plan. It was detailed as detailed could be. The only problem was that there were no floor plans of the inside of the compound. It was an utterly unknown quantity.

'We have had problems with Google Earth, the satellite has real trouble trying to gather information over that part of the planet, whether it be natural causes, or Santa Inc. have strong systems in place to block them. We have however, a member of our team already up there, ex SAS and Fathers For Justice, on the ground. He's covertly taking as many photos of the outside of the compound, stables, sleigh garage and launch pad.'

The projector flashed up a series of photos that were stunning in their quality. Holiday photos they were not.

'I know we're there to destroy Christmas,' said one of the men, Dash, who was smoking a thin cheroot. 'But are we allowed to help ourselves to "the spoils of war" afterwards?'

'No,' said Tom, simply. 'We touch absolutely nothing from that place. Once Mrs. Claus has been captured and killed we are razing it to the ground.'

'But what about the helpers?' Dash continued. 'Can't we adopt them and take them home and have them as our own children?'

Two seconds later Dash was on the floor, the back of his head blown out. The cheroot was still between his lips.

'What we don't need are any bleeding heart liberals making this task harder than it has to be. Anyone who has any second doubts, leave now. You have a thirty second amnesty.' Tom held a gun that looked like a Walther PPK with a silencer screwed onto it. A lithe, wiry chap to Ignatius' left stood up, putting his hands in the air as he rose. 'Don't shoo...' was all he managed to get out, before he too was on the floor as dead as dead can be.

'Fucking deadwood,' Tom growled, putting the gun on the little side table in front of him. And that's when Ignatius knew that they were all going to end up being deadwood, if not during the mission, then by Tom Davis who was very clearly insane.

'Phillip,' Mrs. Claus shouted above the noise as he got out of the snow machine, a small satchel slung over his left shoulder. He raised his hand up in greeting and trudged across the snow towards her. It was when he pulled down the scarf covering his face free that her heart started skipping wildly; her throat seemed to swell up with instantaneous love. He was so *handsome*! Not since she first found herself in the same room as Santa (she still really couldn't remember her life before this) had she felt this giddy. It was in the next heartbeat that it was decided, Mrs. Claus was ready to find love and that Phillip was the man she was going to spend the rest of his life with. She would even split the workload with him over the next fifty Christmases; that would mean that Phillip would potentially live to see another one hundred years. The serum that she gave them to aid longevity, she would send back to the laboratory to see if the helpers could make it a little more powerful, with any luck Mrs. Claus may have one hundred and fifty years of unfettered loving. Yes, the impotence was a slight issue, but there were special roots and barks that Phillip could gnaw on before the act of coitus. If not she could always pick up a bag of Viagra the next time that she left the nth pole. There would be *no* castration. Of that, Mrs. Claus was certain.

The next week, Phillip, or to give him his new name, Santa Seven, was being fattened up, but he was no calf and there would be no slaughtering on Mrs. Claus' watch. The helpers were allowed to see their new Santa through Polaroids only; the first time they would actually meet him would be on Christmas Eve. Sometimes the helpers would land lucky and they would have a great boss. Sadly with Santa Six they had fifty years of a bad egg, they hadn't liked him that much—he used to kick them if they didn't load the sleigh fast enough, and with their "hands", loading was oft a slow and laborious process.

Phillip undertook his new role with great seriousness and ate as much as possible, while taking the thick, black, serum that would help with his longevity. Dish after dish of gyuvetch would be brought to his table, a hearty stew made up from seal, bear and the occasional Reindeer (natural causes only) steak. His beard, which had come out a little too weedily for Mrs. Claus' liking (Phillip did confess to it being his first ever beard) soon began to take hold and had grown into a luxuriant chin mane that would be dyed white as would Phillip's hair on top. Image was *everything*.

And as his belly began to expand, inch by inch, the more Mrs. Claus fell in love with him.

There had been a few more instances where Mrs. Claus ran to the toilet to vomit furiously; she had entertained the thought that there may be a disgruntled helper who was trying to poison her. Unbeknownst to the helpers, one night, when they were all asleep, she installed several hi-def cameras with trip-switch technology in the kitchen in order to catch the nefarious fiend in the act. Then she'd use their skin as ankle socks. Her temper had only ever spiralled out of control on a few occasions; against, of course, the paedophile Santa, and one of the reindeer who somehow broke free of its exoskeletal flight suit and tried to gallop for its freedom. The chase across the never-ending expanse of snow had been great, but in the end, a sudden dip defeated the reindeer and the beast found itself floundering, then met its end as a nineteen stone Mrs. Claus launched herself on top of it and buried a twelve inch carving knife into its skull.

And then there was the time with the parent. The parent who had tried to sue Santa Inc. Mrs. Claus thought it was that instance that had helped to send the first, lovely, amazing Santa shuffling off the mortal coil and leave the business in a state of toxic shock. She *should* have somehow worked through her grief and not have resorted to violence; the police found what was left of the parent in question in five different counties and not all at the same time.

Mrs. Claus hoped with all her heart that Phillip would be the one who would make her soft and cuddly again, that the enormous tsunami of rage that she experienced would become, in time, a gentle lapping of the tide against a pebbly beach. Her stomach gave a sudden, massive, breathtaking twinge; Mrs. Claus had a dread thought that she was going to be sick.

It was just the baby giving her an almighty kick.

It had been a nightmare of a journey to get from the small airstrip one hundred miles away from the Santa Inc. compound, but they were now, according to Tom Davis' calculations, less than five miles away. Ignatius had found the going particularly tough; his body was not one that was built for stamina, duration and longev-ity—he had to give the smokes up as soon as they entered colder air; his lungs felt like they were going to shut down on him with every half-wheeze he managed to get in. His breath rattled like rusty tin cans tied to the bumper of a wedding car. If he got through this and the upcoming onslaught and the crazier by the second Tom, Ignatius promised that he was going to go on the mother of all health kicks and even go down to the gym to try and get himself a six pack, rather than go to the off-licence and buy himself one.

They were all wearing white combat uniforms that had been stolen from a Norwegian Army depot and were traipsing across the snow in lovingly made snowshoes. Each man carried a backpack containing food and spare ammunition—the gun that Ignatius had was a SPK 720 AZ; an automatic machinegun that could melt a hole through a wall quite easily. Ignatius had been over-awed by the amount of impressive firepower Tom brought to the table; Tom had simply said that you would never take a banana to a knife fight.

Once they were only a mile away from the compound, a figure popped his head out of the snow, it was Barry Wood, ex SAS.

'How you been Barry,' Tom asked, lying flat on the snow, looking through a pair of digital zoom binoculars. The compound was in the distance, this is where the final assault would begin from, and it was the most precarious bit of the whole mission, if they were spotted before the charge, then they were all as good as dead.

'It's been fucking cold, let me tell you that for nothing,' Barry replied, his squashed face looked like it was near-black with patches of frostbite. There was one white bit that was shining on his forehead and Ignatius shuddered when he thought it might actually be the bone of Barry's skull.

'Why haven't you been wearing a facemask? You look a right state,' Tom whispered, placing the binoculars on the snow and lying on his side to stare at the tireless campaigner.

'It's not frostbite, this black stuff, it's actually the wool from the balaclava, it got so cold it stuck to my skin and when I managed to get the fucking thing off my head, all these patches of wool had seeped into my fucking skin somehow. Back at the camp I tried to wash and scrub them off, but it looks like the money you're paying will have to go for some deep exfoliation.'

'So, has there been any activity?' Ignatius asked. Everyone looked at him, but nobody said anything.

'Nah, there's been fucking nothing,' Barry said. 'They had the new Santa in a while ago, there's been no sign of him since he entered the compound. Mrs. Claus has only been out once herself, they had a cow flown in by helicopter and as soon as it was out onto the ground and the helicopter flew away she butchered it and took it indoors with her. That's been the last I've seen of her at all. The helpers make the occasional venture outdoors, but I think that's just for the occasional breath of fresh air. I think sustained exposure to this cold would kill them extremely quickly.' Bob reached into his coat pocket and pulled out a Mars Bar. He unwrapped it quickly and took a massive bit out of it. 'So how long before we hit the compound?'

'Now,' said Tom, who bade two of the team to him. They passed to him two sections of tubing, which he fitted together and it looked like a very basic rocket launcher. He then attached a small black box with a USB sticking out of it and it beeped sharply a couple of times as it came to life. He then went into his backpack and retrieved a small ball, sickly grey in colour and popped it into the tube.

'This is what replaces a rocket these days, boys,' he smiled sharply and his eyes seemed to bulge in their sockets. 'We're here because we all hate Christmas, and that we've been done over by this fucking greedy corporation for too long. Santa Inc. has ridiculed and taunted us, made us feel less like the true men that we really are. Let's burn everything into the fucking ground.'

The men made their final approach, and once the compound was finally in sight, a tall, proud building that dominated the skyline, Tom hefted the launcher onto his shoulder, pressed a button on the control pad and after a series of beeps that got faster in pace and higher in pitch, one long continuous beep prompted that the launcher was ready to wreak havoc.

'So Santa, at the end of this week, I'm going to get the jet to take us on a round the world journey, just so that you have a notion of what is involved on the night. Of course there will be the usual potions and magic in place to make sure that you do the job as quickly as possible and cause as little disturbance also. There will be a six week course coming up in how to break into people's houses, less and less people use chimney's nowadays, so it's much easier to pick a lock and sneak around.' Mrs. Claus was standing by the fireplace, letting the heat warm her backside. She looked at Phillip with such unfettered joy. He had turned out to be absolutely magnificent. He sat there, in the large wooden throne that the original Santa had hand carved all of those years ago, and for an instant, just one instant, all thoughts of the original Santa had vanished from Mrs. Claus' mind

'Why thank you my dear!' Santa Seven bellowed, his large, not the least bit timorous voice, booming and reverberating the oak beams above them. 'I'm sure that when the time comes I will carry out my duties with aplomb and panache!'

With every day that passed Santa and Phillip were drifting further and further apart until the day would come when Santa would never have known an existence before he set foot on the nth Pole snow. Sometimes his pre-Santa life came to him in his dreams, he was usually a young copper, his first days on the beat, running the streets, arresting criminals and then afterwards down the pub with his new colleagues, playing pool and smoking Benson and Hedges until the air turned blue with smoke.

'Santa, would you like to share my bed with me this evening?' Mrs. Claus asked meekly. Santa Seven looked startled, and then looked down at his red trousers, there was some twitchy, erratic movement down there, after so, so many years. Santa grinned. Then the far wall, on which hung the stuffed head of the very first scientifically engineered Reindeer, Adolf, who'd had a neon pink nose, exploded in a mass of masonry, metal antlers and flame. Mrs. Claus was thrown across the room by the impact, and luckily landed on the sofa. Santa was just pushed back into his chair, and would have survived if it hadn't been for a foot long piece of steel that was slightly bent and whickered across the room at tremendous speed and looked like it would go back the way it came, as it was boomerang shaped. Sadly, Santa Seven's face got in the way of it and went in left of his nose and came out the back of his skull in a millisecond.

Mrs. Claus' ears rang; her vision came and went like a fast zoom lens. Another explosion, this time hitting another part of the compound. She tried to push herself up, to see what all the nonsense was, to get Santa away and to safety, but then her legs felt wet like she had pissed herself and was followed quickly by a massive pain in her lower stomach. Mrs. Claus blacked out.

'Attack!' Tom screamed, dropping the launcher on the ground and bringing his machine gun into the mix. In front of them, from small trap doors in the ground came the helpers and the attackers actually paused with terror. It was the first time that any of them, bar Barry, had actually seen one of Santa Inc's infamous and hidden workers, and now they had, they all wished they hadn't. Seven heavily armed men against what looked like a small army of imps of the perverse. Ignatius felt his heart trying to escape from his mouth, he saw his demise coming much sooner than he had imagined.

They were small, but not small enough as to be midgets, but around the size of a tall six year old. They had long arms, and the hands had been replaced somehow with cutting and hammering tools. How they ate, Ignatius could only fathom at. Their faces were swarthy, and when they opened their mouths, they were full of thousands of tiny razor sharp teeth. They had small metal boxes grafted onto their throats. From these came unearthly screams and wails. They wore the most basic of clothes, hessian sacks that had been dyed red and green, keeping in with the spirit of Christmas. And they ran towards the seven men en masse.

'Open fire!' Tom screamed and the seven men cut down a good number of the helpers, but still more were coming from the holes in the floor. The screams they made the men think they were in a cattle mart. The air soon began to stink of cordite, not unpleasant, but heavy. The men had nothing to fear because as soon as they were reloading and firing again, the helpers hadn't advanced in the slightest. They looked scarier than they actually were.

Ignatius had never fired a gun before now and was surprised at how natural it all was, how the heat seeped through his thick gloves and seemed to attack his very bones. He loved it. He could feel the presence of his dead wife and children standing next to him cheering him on, and he broke out into a grin. He began to laugh as he took the tops of heads off of a row of three helpers.

The men approached the massive hole in the side of the building and continued to fire round after round. Hundreds of bodies littered the area and the snow was completely red.

It was another bolt of pain that brought Mrs. Claus back to. She dragged herself towards Santa's chair and began to scream when she saw how dead he was. Fury like nothing else consumed her, and she got up on both feet, unmindful of the strange pain that seemed to want to bring her to her knees every few minutes, there would be time to fix shrapnel wounds later if that's what it was. She looked down at her legs, her dress was becoming slightly tattered, and her legs were sticky with fluid. Whoever it was that had killed her Santa *and* made her piss herself was soon going to find out the true meaning of "last moment terror". With strength ebbing from her she ran through to the munitions room and picked up the pulse rifle and her bowie knife. That's all she needed.

'Ignatius,' Tom said softly to him, the first time Tom had actually spoken to him since the briefing in Scotland. 'Go round the back of the building and take care of the reindeer. They'll all be in the stables, just a bullet to the back of their heads will fix them up, and then come back quickly.'

'Yes Sir,' Ignatius said and dashed off, half-expecting to be cut down by his comrades as he ran. But no, he was round the corner and thought that he must actually have played his part well and killed the required quota of helpers not to become deadwood himself. As he approached the stables the hysterical braying was almost enough to go back and face Tom and plead with him for someone else to do it. There were about ten of them and they were each in their individual pens and kicking against the doors with their hind legs, trying to get out. Their exoskeletal suits were cutting into their hides due to the frantic nature and strange postures they were putting their bodies through. He raised the gun to mow them down when all of a sudden it seemed that the very air he breathed had been sucked out of him. Everything went bright white, compounded by the pureness of the snow, but even though he was wearing dark shades he still had to cover his eyes against the intenseness of the light. Then everything smelt of barbeques. He left the reindeer be who were going utterly bananas now, Ignatius thought that a couple of them might actually escape, but more power to them if they did. He ran back to his team.

Well, what was left of his team.

Which was nothing.

Maybe a small puddle of blood.

But nothing else.

Mrs. Claus' pulse rifle had put paid to that merry ragtag of usurpers.

Mrs. Claus pressed a button on the gun and the magazine fell to the ground. She looked at the newcomer with momentary inquisi-tiveness; knew from files that she kept that it was Ignatius Solomon, nothing but a loser and someone who would never have become Santa, even if his wife and children had survived. She knew scum when she saw it and she knew how to deal with scum. She threw the gun down and grinned, reaching into the waist belt of her skirt and retrieved the knife and started to walk very slowly towards the man who hated Christmas.

Ignatius felt calm. He could mow her down before she got to him, but he wanted to see her approach, felt that he needed to see the monster that had destroyed his chances of ever to coming to peace with Christmas. But had she really destroyed them? If it hadn't been for the refusal he would never have found himself in the nth pole. So maybe he had found peace, but had just come to it in another, more final way.

'You evil, evil man!' Mrs. Claus shrilled at Ignatius. She was infuriated by the fact that he wasn't trying to run away from her. He didn't even seem scared. She started running across the snow, she wasn't that far, maybe fifteen steps and she'd have him. She didn't notice him slowly lifting up the machine pistol. Then a scream burst forth from her lips and she fell back. A white hot searing pain was coming from between her legs, she felt a tearing down there that seemed to travel all the way up her back. She tried to get up but couldn't feel below her waist. She managed to prop herself up on her hands took look down at herself. A hand was coming out from under her dress. Then the arm. And then, with another almighty rip, the other hand, then arm appeared. The lower half of Mrs. Claus was being wrenched about furiously. She stared at the thing (*her child!*) as the head appeared. It had pure white hair, flecked with bits of blood. Then with another tug it was free from her and Mrs. Claus could only look with wonder and terror as the thing thrashed about in the snow. She tried to think back to the last time she and the original Santa had had sex. It just wasn't possible it had been hundreds of years ago. Had one of the helpers broke in one night when she was drunk and raped her? How had something that big grown in her and she hadn't shown? Not one little bit? How...

The world came to a sudden, crashing, stop as Ignatius emptied his magazine into her chest.

Ignatius approached the child with something akin to wonder. It was lying on its back, still crying, pissing into the air. It was about the size of a ten year old. It had white down covering its face and it had a pot belly.

It stopped bawling when it saw Ignatius and they both held each other's gaze for the longest of times.

Ignatius took the knife from Mrs. Claus' clenched fist and cut through the umbilical cord that was as thick as a ship's rope. Once the knife was discarded, he picked up her offspring, surprised at its heft. Baby Santa snuggled into the nape of Ignatius' neck. It was incredibly still.

Ignatius went into the ruins of the compound and walked up the staircase until he came to Mrs. Claus' bedroom. He placed the wide-eyed, curious and bearded child onto the bed and looked for some clothes for it to wear. He pulled out from the wardrobe the Santa suit for Santa Two, who sadly hadn't filled out as much as Mrs. Claus would have liked. Ignatius looked at it and thought it would be a little big for even this outsize infant, but that he would soon grow into it.

He dressed the newborn slowly, the memories of him slowly dressing his own children came flooding back, hurting him. Ignatius started to cry.

'Daddy?' baby Santa croaked. He sounded like a teenager with a breaking voice.

'Yes, I am your Daddy,' Ignatius said to baby Santa as he tickled his little one under the chin.

CURE

'IT'S BAD NEWS,' the Doctor said, sympathetic eyes, mouth slightly turned down like a child who has been forbidden sweets for drawing on the wallpaper. 'The tests have all come back and they reveal that you have Stage 2B bone cancer. That means that you have a high grade which has grown through the bone wall. We will of course start a treatment of aggressive chemotherapy and try to catch it before the disease progresses to Stage 3. That's when it spreads to other parts of your body.'

Charlotte started to cry. The Doctor opened his drawer and pulled out a box of tissues which he passed across to her. As he waited for the sobbing to end he thought about what clothes he should take with him for his dirty little weekend away with Elspeth, the woman he had met in a wine bar the previous week. Then something else went off in his head, and it troubled him. He started at Charlotte hard, for the longest of times, and then spoke again.

'There is another treatment which has been developed in Sweden, this will be highly controversial, ethically unsound and when news reaches the public there will be hell to pay. The storm that this treatment will create will never die down, mark my words. In the five tests that have been carried out it has nevertheless proven one-hundred percent effective. So to be eligible for this test you have to be diagnosed with Stage 2B, which you have, and you must also sign a contract between yourself and the treatment centre whereby you declare you will never, ever talk about what you see, hear or experience while in their care. And the day it's exposed, you'll have to go into hiding forever.'

'One hundred percent effective. You mean a cure for cancer?'

The doctor nodded, then opened up his drawer and pulled out a brown A4 folder and passed it across to her.

'All the information you need is here. Do *not* show this to anybody.'

Charlotte left the doctor's and walked down the street until she reached a vegan cafe where she had carrot cake and drank a cup of green tea. Her bones felt hollow, her eyes seemed to shrink back into her skull. The cake tasted like ash in her mouth and no amount of tea seemed to be able to wash it away. Her stomach felt heavy and bloated, her lymph nodes felt like they were going to burn through her skin.

She phoned her mother while she was on the train and said that she was coming home. Mother was oblivious to the worried and near hysterical tone of her daughter's voice and said that she would put some dinner on and that Father would be really happy to see her, he had found a couple of books in a second hand store that he thought she would be interested in.

Nobody was waiting to pick her up when the train pulled into Effingham station, but there was a taxi there.

When the taxi pulled up at the house she saw her mother in the garden. She got out, paid the driver and he took her small bag of luggage from the boot and handed it to her. All of a sudden it seemed impossibly heavy to carry. Her mother looked up, smiled and came to greet her. Then the world tilted sideways and Charlotte went with it.

When she came to, the faces of her worried parents peered down at her.

'What's wrong, bubblegum?' her father soothed stroking her face.

Charlotte tried to get up, but she felt smothered by the blanket they had placed on her. It felt heavy and it was suffocating, suffocating her.

She blacked out again.

Much later, sitting in the kitchen she told them the diagnosis. She sat there, unable to cry as she devastated her parents. They asked her about what treatment she would go on and she told them that she would start a course of chemotherapy as soon as the hospital had done some more tests.

Charlotte stayed with them for a couple of days and let herself be spoiled and pampered. She sat with them, trying her hardest to seem interested as they went for a meal by the riverside. Her mind was far, far away, running through every little bit of information that the doctor had given her.

Her father dropped her off at the train station and there were many tears as she boarded the city-bound train. Both parents had been poleaxed by the further announcement that Charlotte was going to hole herself away in a treatment centre in Sweden and that they wouldn't be allowed to come and visit, but were allowed to send letters and phone. When her mother had asked why, she said that it was the only way she could do it—the only way she could be strong was if she did it on her own.

Charlotte booked a flight to Sweden—and once she had landed, hired a car and drove to Ytterby, a small village on the island of Resarö. The medical centre was next to the church.

She checked in at reception and was taken through to her room—it was comfortable, with a single bed, sofa, TV and a fridge. She walked a lot in those first few days, trying to empty her head from thoughts of her disease. Sometimes she felt as if she could feel her bones being eaten by increments.

On the third day she was called through to the office of her case doctor, a tall, blonde man called Stephan whose eyes were the bluest she had ever seen.

'So you have read the literature,' he said in a sing-song voice. It wasn't a question; it was a statement of fact.

'Yes, I did, but this was a very hard sell on my parents. They think I've gone and joined some holistic health farm.'

'Of course, they will naturally be worried. You say you are their only child? Then, of course I trust you have told them they can still phone and email you? You can Skype them if you wish, but you must never reveal anything below shoulder height. Nobody must know that you're showing.'

'Yes I have, and I will abide by every rule. I just want to get better.'

Stephan smiled and held out a clenched fist. He opened it and revealed a single yellow and red capsule; to Charlotte it reminded her of the rhubarb and custard sweets of her childhood.

'You take this pill Charlotte, swallow it and that's all the medication that you need. Then we will move onto the next phase.'

Charlotte stared at the pill and half expected it to combust in front of her eyes. Could the cure for cancer really be this simple? She reached out and took it, popped it into her mouth and dry swallowed it. Stephan winced.

'I can never do that myself, always need a chaser!' he exclaimed, rifling through the sheaf of papers in front of him. 'Now, if I'm correct it will be in the next day or so when we can commence with the second part of the treatment. This part is wholly up to you Charlotte, it depends on your success. The window is very small, as you well know.' Stephan got up, flashing a smile. His teeth were very white.

Charlotte stared at herself in the mirror, carefully applying mascara. She had enquired about artificial insemination, but due to the possibility of bleeding after the procedure it was against protocol.

She walked the half mile into the town centre and found a bar and waited. It took her a while to find someone who spoke English. His name was Jorge, and he was very beautiful and very intense. She went back with him to his sparsely furnished flat and slept with him. She lied when she said they would see each other again. The walk back to the medical centre was one of the longest she had ever taken. He had been nice, and it would have been fun to have seen him again. That day her body screamed in agony with the pain from her exertions.

On the last day of her cycle she took a pregnancy test. Stephan was happy. Charlotte was moved from the room to her own flat on the outskirts of town. Her food and other sundries were delivered to her twice a week. She went out for small walks, only to get some fresh air, nothing more. She phoned her family once a week and told them she was doing well. Her father asked her why her hair hadn't fallen out. He then broke down, begging her not to try any holistic medicines; that it wasn't right for his daughter to die before he did.

Charlotte's stomach grew big with her pregnancy, very big. During the last month one of the nurses came to stay with her. Charlotte was an utter wreck by this time, barely eating, sleeping for twenty hours a day; she looked like a Western version of an Ethiopian famine victim. The nurse was concerned that she might not make it and so Stephan came over. *It will be fine*, he said, *I've seen worse cases than this. She'll be fine.*

Her waters broke and she was rushed to hospital, the pain was like nothing she had ever experienced and Charlotte thought that she might die, and if she did, well, it wouldn't be that bad a deal. She wanted her dad to be there, holding her hand, talking her through it—but all she got were several people clad in green scrubs with masks over their faces, their eyes emotionless.

'Push,' she was told.

And so she pushed. And pushed.

All of a sudden the pain was gone and she felt swallowed up by a vacuum. She saw one of the attendants hold up her baby, but it wasn't her baby, it was a dirty grey sac, flecked with blood. But she could see movement within the sac; her baby was pushing and kicking. *What was happening?* she moaned.

The attendant laid the sac on the table and cut it open with a pair of surgical scissors. Thick black liquid flooded out from the sac, and then Charlotte knew that something was severely wrong even though she was told that her cure for cancer would only come when she fell pregnant, that if she didn't fall pregnant she would die.

The attendant smiled as she lifted the baby up, and Charlotte started to scream when she saw that the baby had no eyes, no ears, no mouth or nose. The arms were devoid of hands and the legs had no tiny feet, but they kicked back and forth, feebly.

Stephan came into the room, nodded to the attendant who took the baby away and he placed a hand on her shoulder.

'That was your cancer, Charlotte. Your cancer. You're cured.'

THE TIP RUN

A S SATURDAY TRADITIONS went, it was never the best, but under the circumstances it was all they had.

Saturday was tip day.

Dad would wake Steve up at around eight, always being careful not to make too much noise as Saturday morning was always the morning Mum stayed in bed, sleeping off what was known in the house as the "bitch of a hangover". It was always Dad's turn to sleep the "bitch" off on the Sunday.

Living so far away from the nearest town or even one of Steve's school friends meant that tip day was the only weekend entertainment going, unless Mum would realise late afternoon that there was hardly anything in the house and they would drive through twenty miles of rather treacherous countryside to reach Fine Fayre at Galaston. And only very occasionally would there be chance to watch a late-night Hammer horror film. Apart from these brief forays, Steve's weekends would be uneventful. Being an only child meant they always were.

The tip was only a three mile drive and they would always get there before other hopeful treasure-seekers arrived.

Dad had always said that it seemed to him that it was a strange place to situate a council-run tip; the only reason he could think of its being there, situated at the lowest part of the Stour valley, was that on hot days the stink wouldn't carry.

Now dressed and full of buttered toast and sweet tea, the pair set off in the burgundy-coloured Triumph Herald, leaving the gravel drive with the hump of grass running down the centre of it and turning left onto the narrow country road, flanked on both sides by weather-beaten and moss covered dykes, driving towards the magnificent Pennywell Hills that overshadowed the whole of the Stour Valley.

They stopped off at Graham's farm and Dad quickly got out to buy a dozen eggs and some thick-cut bacon that would have been prepared only the day before. Graham wasn't around, for which Steve was silently thankful; on many an occasion he would have to wait in the car for a good hour, sometimes longer as the two men chomped down on the week's (non) events.

But today there was only Vera, Graham's sullen and never happy wife, so Dad was back in under five minutes, the bacon wrapped up in thick greaseproof paper, the eggs in a rather beaten up looking egg box. He put the bacon in a bag in the boot which was supposed to keep things cool, but Steve had his suspicions that it never did.

Arriving at the tip, whoever had opened it up had disappeared somewhere; they found no-one else there. As there was no car park, they had driven into the tip itself. Father and son both got out, smiling at each other and they went to the boot of the car, taking out two pairs of gloves, one pair large, the other pair small, and two bags, both large.

While regulations were slowly starting to kill off the amount of stuff you could find and take—the council's becoming wise to the fact that they could get any found wares first and sell them on to fill their already overflowing coffers, the Stour Valley Refuse Centre was as gnarly and as boots on as it came; no matter what you found it was *yours*, be it an empty can of baked beans or an undiscovered Picasso. If somebody did happen to be working on site on the Saturday (the only day it was open to the public) you might have to pay him a couple of quid to help with that evening's beer money—but usually it was free.

And what treasures! The tip had always been good to the pair of them—never being a family of much means—Dad worked selling insurance and Mum cooked at an old folk's home—the tip had given up such troves as pocket watches, medals and once a book that Steve had found and Dad had driven down to London with—a full two day's journey. When he came back he gave Steve a five pound note. Steve overheard his Dad saying to Mum that the book had fetched hundreds. Hundreds of what though, Steve didn't know.

There had been several strange finds. Last year, on his seventh birthday, Steve had found a box of dolls eyes (eyelashes attached) and a carrier bag of false teeth, partials and full sets.

Dad told Steve that they would meet each other in half an hour, go through what they had found then have another half an hour's rummaging before going home. Steve nodded, put on his gloves, the thick material rasping against his skin and flexed his hands inside them. He hefted the canvas bag over his shoulder and made his way into the tip.

Of course, there were rules that Steve had to abide by.

1: *NEVER climb anything higher than you.*

2: *If it looked heavy, it WAS heavy and would probably crush you if it fell on you.*

3: *Don't pick up any dead animals*

4: *Fridges and Freezers—NEVER EVER climb into them.*

Simple rules to follow—though the first time they went to the skip when Steve was six he conveniently forgot the first rule and started to climb up a ten foot mound of rubbish. He had been using a metal pole, the white paint on it flaking off, to help prop himself up with—as he stabbed it deep into the mound to heave himself up further he heard a sharp crunching sound. He tried to pull the pole out; it was suddenly very heavy. When he finally freed it from the heap he stared with blank incomprehension at the illegal trap that had bit deeply into the pole, near severing it in half. It wasn't until much later that he realised it that it could have been his foot that ended up in the trap.

Ever since that day Steve spent his time at the small piles of debris that surrounded the bigger mounds, picking through the slowly deteriorating polythene bags and wet and mouldy cardboard boxes.

Today Steve only had one thing on his mind. It was going to be Dad's birthday in a few days and while Mum had already bought a bottle of aftershave (Brut, *every* man's favourite) on his behalf, he really wanted to find something that would knock his dad's socks off.

He wandered deep into the tip, gazing up at the truly mammoth mountains of trash that surrounded him. Sometimes he wondered what it would be like if it all collapsed and he had to swim his way back to the Triumph. Then he'd imagine creatures crawling out of the rubbish, eyeless monsters which could only use their acute sense of smell to get around, and towards the only things they really liked to tear apart with their razor sharp teeth—eight year old boys...

'You okay there, son?' His Dad's voice was crisp, clear and loud. Steve cupped his gloved hands over his mouth and yelled back that he was fine.

'Good,' Dad shouted back. In the distance Steve could hear the low sound of an approaching motor. He thought he had better get a move on and get finding.

He came to a broken pile of furniture; chairs, what appeared to be a kitchen table with lovely looking thistles carved into the legs, numerous shelves and a chest of drawers that was lying on its back, covered in dried orange paint. He opened up the two smaller drawers, seeing only newspaper lining the bottom. He took the newspaper out from each and looked at the yellowed sheets, hoping to find a cartoon strip to read. The two larger drawers came out easily and yielded nothing. Steve grasped the turned knobs of the bottom drawer and tried to tug it towards him. It wouldn't budge. He got on the chest, knowing that his dad wouldn't be upset—nothing for him to get trapped by here! He knelt down, grabbed the painted white knobs again and yanked with all of his might. The drawer came out a few inches and that was it, but Steve decided he wouldn't give up, he heard a rattling as he pulled. Jumping off the drawers he looked around the piles and his face lit up with joy as he saw a very heavy looking crowbar that had been jammed through h the top of the head of a manne-quin. He pulled the dark blue metal bar out from the head, splitting its face in half.

The bar was heavy but he gamefully wedged it into the gap the drawer gave him and pushed down on it. Almost instantly the wood of the drawer gave way, Steve fell forward and a splinter of wood ripped his jeans and cut the skin around his knee. He let out a short gasp of pain and sat down on the drawers, pulling back the material of his dark blue denims and inspecting the cut. His bot-tom lip trembled slightly, but he took a deep breath in and closed his eyes. It wasn't all that bad. He got up and stamped his foot down on the ground, he felt a thin trickle run down his leg and into his sock. Nothing that a swab of Dettol and a plaster wouldn't fix, though the thought of Mum wiping his knee with it made him wince.

He looked at the broken drawer. He didn't feel too guilty. It didn't really belong to anyone, but somebody might have been able to take the paint off. He crouched down and put his hand into the space and felt about. His fingers slid against something, he then grabbed it, pulled it out and looked intently at his find.

It was an old cardboard box and written on it was "HARDY PERFECT" and a picture of a fishing reel. He opened the top of the box carefully, the reel was there, nestled safely amongst the origi-nal oil paper packaging. The reel had a cream handle made of ivory.

Steve grinned, his Dad was a keen fisherman and this was just the best thing he could ever find him. On his first sweep of the tip, too!

He put the top back on the box carefully, and ran back through the tip to the entrance to wait for his Dad.

Steve suddenly skidded to a stop. There was a white van in front of the Triumph and the back doors were open. He *tried* to take in the scene before him, but he couldn't. Dad was lying on the ground, his eyes shut, his face covered in blood. A tall man with broad shoulders, wearing a filthy army jacket and corduroy trousers had his Dad by the legs and stepped into the van, trying to drag the unconscious man in.

Steve dropped the box onto the ground and ran towards his Dad, screaming. The tall man looked up and he yanked Steve's Dad into the back of the van hard, his head meeting the tow ball on the way in with an almighty thud. Steve came to the van and grabbed at his Dad's shoulders, but his gloved hands failed to grasp onto the polyester material of his jacket. The tall man's eyes flashed, almost with amusement, as he pushed Steve hard, and he fell back onto the dirt.

'I *found* him, he's *mine*,' the tall man said simply. He took off his army jacket, revealing a white short sleeved shirt and a tie with a Santa Claus on it, even though it was six months away from Christmas. The man paused for a second, thinking. He jumped out of the van walked towards Steve and knelt down by him, ruffled his hair and kissed his forehead gently. His breath stunk of dirt.

He walked towards the boxed fishing reel, picked it up and placed it between the boy's splayed legs. Ruffling Steve's hair again he left him, jumped into the back of the van, slammed the doors shut from the inside and seconds later the van tore out of the tip as Steve screamed and screamed until the next treasure seeker arrived, thirty minutes later.

HEAD SOUP

BEARING IN MIND that Peter was in his mid-eighties, Matthew thought that he had sounded reasonably alert when they arranged the interview for the following day.

'By all means,' Peter chortled heartily when Matthew coyly asked if he could bring a couple of books with him for the elder man to sign. 'I'm just glad that there are people out there who still like my work!'

Peter Van Basel was a horror writer of Germanic descent, long retired from the game. He had written over fifty novels and had released six collections and was named editor to over twice as many horror and supernatural anthologies. What was undeniably true about the man was that his novels, especially the *Pulsing Blood* trilogy, were amongst some of the most imaginative work that had come out of the British Isles since the end of the first war. His star was a bright one, and he was the Guest of Honour at many conventions the world over and was most cordial indeed, always making time for his many fans who adored him with the simple affection more often held for a close relative.

Then in the late eighties a short story he had written was published in The 3rd Leopard Book of Horror Stories, entitled *Head-Soup for the Hole*. It was neither the best he had written nor a slip in form—Fearzone Magazine had simply called it 'workmanlike.'

Six months later, Mr Johann Rutgers, thirty-five and from Frankfurt am Main, Germany, was put on trial for cooking his wife's head at the local PTA meeting and serving the soup he had made from it. Three of the teachers had drunk it to no immediate physical ill effect. In fact, Johann would probably have gotten away with it if the Art teacher, a morbidly obese lady named Diana Bonn hadn't bumped into the table on her return for more soup, and knocked the copper pot off onto the floor, revealing all.

On the first day of his trial, when asked why he did such a thing, Johann said that Peter's story had spoken to him and had got into his head so much; that it *made* him kill his wife and cook her head like it had been written in the tale. Apart from one wry comment in a newspaper that Johann's ending was a much better one than the author of the story had depicted, there was universal condemnation and outcry that such a thing could happen. Leopard Publishing missed the boat completely and said they would be removing all copies from the stores immediately and pulping them. The copies that had got out were passed around schoolyards and work canteens. Specialist genre bookshops were then rumoured to be selling second hand copies for one hundred and twenty pounds plus.

Newspapers crucified him, and no matter how many interviews Peter gave defending his right to write, and to not have any moral obligation to people who clearly manifested deep seated mania, the damage was done. Peter's career was ruined. His next book, *Louisa Kibble Is Always Dead* was refused shelf space by John Menzies and after that his publisher and agent dumped him within the space of a week. Apart from a few short stories in fledgling fanzines, Peter faded from public view. He was very rich, the money earned during his writing career was supplemental; there was old money from his family and he would never have to work again, but when the choice to work had been taken away from him, he decided that he would never write another word of fiction.

There had been one, small article that briefly said that he had married his partner Maria in a small ceremony in Kent, but apart from that, he was as good as dead.

Matthew Jolks had been a fan of Peter's work ever since he was thirteen years old and had read his short story *No Nightfall for the*

Guilty in a very obscure anthology that had been published by Ember Books in 1963. The young Matthew had found it at a Bring and Buy sale and was instantly captivated by the hellish cover of a woman being eaten alive by demons. On the whole, the stories in the anthology were pretty weak, but Peter's story had grabbed him by the throat and refused to let go. Matthew read the book until the covers were bent and worn and the spine was cracked and finally, the pages started to fall out. No matter how many copies Matthew had found in the subsequent years (only five—as it had become another one of those rare collector's copies) he could never bring himself to throw out the original Bring and Buy purchase.

Bounding from job to job after he had left school, he got married, got a job slicing fish in the local Loch Fyne factory, then lost his wife and his job—so at the age of thirty, Matthew found himself working part time in the local supermarket and going back to his teenage love of horror books and running a small fanzine called 'Sliced'. Although it was on the extreme outer fringes of the UK horror field—it had a relatively loyal following. As editor, he refused to go down the route of many publications by trying to source interviews with the talent of the here and now—he was more interested in talking to the actors, authors and other people in the genre who had slipped from the radar altogether.

Such the case had been with Peter Van Basel. He had spent the last five years ever since the fanzine began exhausting every possible avenue in his search for him. Matthew had managed to track down Peters' last known address and had fired a letter off, knowing it to be pretty much a dead end. He had written on the back of the envelope 'If Peter does not live here, please open letter and reply to address,' and sure enough two weeks later, a lovely letter from a female named Gladys confirmed that the former occupants of the house had left in the mid-nineties and had unfortunately left no forwarding address.

Matthew had also tried all of his contacts two, three times over and while they all agreed that an interview with the great man and a re-assessment of his works was well overdue, no-one had any inkling of where he might be. Even his old agent, Louisa Pugh who at the age of ninety-three had made a surprise appearance at one of the many conventions that Matthew attended, admitted that she hadn't heard anything since she had dropped him.

About to give up, Matthew then had a spark of an idea that was the ultimate shot to nothing, but a shot it was, nevertheless. He headed the advert 'van Basel', took a line from the very first story he had read of Peter's and with his name and telephone number under the quotation sent the advert to every regional newspaper in Britain which took a lot of time and a considerable amount of money which he didn't really have to execute.

It was a shot to nothing.

But it hit its mark.

Three weeks after he had sent the mass advert out, he was working hard in the office, editing an interview he had recently conducted with a screenwriter who had produced some cracking scripts, which had been turned into some truly abysmal films. The phone rang, and he leant across his cheap pine writing desk and picked it up.

'Hello there, Matthew Jolks speaking, how can I help you?'

The accent on the other end of the line was cheerful and chirpy.

'Hello Matthew, my name is Peter Van Basel. I saw a rather obscure message in the Effingham Chronicle a few weeks back, and wondered why someone had printed my name and the first line from *No Nightfall*. Being rather nosey in nature, I thought that I couldn't ignore it and not be able to find out what you wanted. So, spill the beans Matthew!'

Peter Van Basel! Found at last! His heart was jumping for joy, and although Peters' jovial tone set the younger man's mind at ease, when he tried to speak, he found himself stuttering over his words.

'It's...amm...amaz...to...' he could only manage to get out.

Peter chuckled kindly.

'Slow down, old chap. Take your time. Mick Jagger had the same effect on me when I met him in the seventies.'

Matthew slowed down and explained all about the *Sliced* fanzine—Peter had never heard of it, but liked the title—and that Matthew had slowly built up a portfolio of interviews, but always mourned the fact that he had never been able to 'interview the greatest British Horror Writer ever.'

The two men chatted on the phone for over an hour; Matthew the fan with an in-depth knowledge of all of Peter's work and Peter would release nuggets of gold into the conversation, telling him how such characters as the famous Popsy Boyd came into being.

'So... this interview,' Peter drawled, a slight tiredness creeping into his voice. 'How would you like to do it?'

'Well we could do it by email...'

'No computer, I'm afraid. Could never get into them. I typed all of my manuscripts.

'Or we could do it by snail mail, or we can see how we get on together, phone each other a few times and if you feel comfortable, we can arrange a face-to-face interview.'

There was a slight pause, and Matthew could hear Peter talk to someone else.

'I think a face-to-face would be the best course of action, young man. If you can come round for some dinner tomorrow, meet my darling wife Maria and then we'll get down to the interview afterwards and roll you onto the last train home?'

'Excuse me?' Matthew was taken aback by the abruptness of the invitation.

'Tomorrow. You live in London?'

'Yes... Seven Sisters.'

'It's only a short skip and a hop to get you here to Effingham-on -the-Stour. My friend, there is no time like the present. Would you like to come and visit us?'

Matthew accepted then with his face burning extremely red, asked, 'I don't mean to sound cheeky, but would it be okay if I brought a few books with me for you to sign?'

'By all means, I'm just glad that there are people out there who still like my work!' Peter chortled heartily, as the older man gave Matthew his address and telephone number just in case anything should happen.

'And one other thing,' Peter almost whispered, 'you won't tell anyone about this just yet? If we are to engineer my return to writing—let's just make sure we get a good interview in the bag first, you understand?'

Matthew didn't, and he *wanted* to phone everyone he knew, but out of respect for the old man, agreed not to go shouting that he was the one to have re-discovered Peter Von Basel. Time enough would come for that. The two men hung up, Peter smiling at his wife and saying that tomorrow should be quite fun, do we have any cakes in dear? and Matthew jumping around the room in glee, trying his hardest not to squeal with delight like a little girl.

The next day, with a bag containing a digital recorder, a bottle of whisky and eight books and several stills from a film that Peter had written the screenplay for, for him to sign, Matthew boarded the tube and took it down to Victoria Station, where he would then jump on the train to Effingham. The bottle of whisky was a gift, but it was all that Matthew could do not to open it and have a drink to settle his nerves. He wondered if this was the same feeling people had when they met royalty. He wondered if Peter would be nervous, then chuckled to himself. Peter was probably past caring about all of this, and only wanted to do the interview for a bit of company, have someone fawn over him other than his wife for a couple of hours.

Sitting on the train, he pulled out his limited edition slip-cased copy of *She Bites*, a collection of stories edited by Selwyn Barker and flicked through it, settling down to read *Sticking Your Head Out is Dangerous*, a story that Peter had written under his pseudonym Eliza Daye, and it had caused quite a lot of outrage when it had first been published. It was about a young woman who loses her head while sticking it out of a train window. While the mother is going crazy with grief, a kindly man in a grey suit goes to find the missing head...

It had been one of those stories that had always felt out of place in the Basel oeuvre. Matthew had always wanted to ask about this story, why Peter had felt the need to write it—because it was a story that had none of the finesse that even some of his more "out there" stories had. Maybe the only reason Eliza had been invented. Matthew had certainly not been able to track down any other Daye stories in other anthologies.

After he had finished the story, he got up and got himself a cup of coffee from the buffet car and drank slowly, savouring the bitterness, but knowing that the caffeine wouldn't do his nerves any good.

Matthew grinned as he noticed that his hands were trembling. Packing the hardback book carefully back into his bag, he closed his eyes and let the train take the last ten minutes into Effingham.

Getting off the train, he looked around the unfamiliar station for the exit. He never trusted train toilets as a rule, and splash catastrophe wasn't a look he wanted to present to Peter and his wife. The feel of the place was actually rather nice as far as railway stations went. Even though the heat was *searing*, people looked more relaxed than they were back in London. Maybe the fresh countrified air was helping to slow everyone down, Matthew thought to himself as he passed a bland branded coffee house, and left the station, walking towards the taxi rank.

He approached the first black cab he saw, and opened up the back door, getting in and dumping his heavy bag on the seat.

'Where you wanting to go to, mate?' the cabbie, a rough looking bloke with a toupee and deathly grey skin asked, starting up the engine.

'Can you take me to Goldstone Place please?' Matthew asked.

'Of course, mate. Nice area up there, who are you going to see?' the driver asked pulling out of the rank and driving out onto the street and into the busy traffic.

'An author. Used to be kinda well known back in the day, but has now slipped into obscurity. You wouldn't have heard of him.' Matthew then pulled his iphone headphones from his pocket and jammed them into his ears before the taxi driver asked him who the author was.

The taxi wove its way through the town centre traffic and was soon driving through the leafy suburbs of Effingham. After another ten minutes and just out onto the fringes of the countryside, they pulled up at the gates of what looked like to be a walled estate. Paying the cabbie his fare, Matthew got out and pressed the button on the intercom. After a few seconds it crackled into life. A lady spoke.

'Yes?'

'Hello? I'm Matthew Jolks and I've come to talk to Peter van Basel. I believe he's expecting me?'

'Yes of course! Stand back a few steps please!'

The electronic gates began to buzz and then one of them lurched open, nearly knocking Matthew over onto his back. Grinning, he hefted his bag over his shoulder and started to walk down the tree lined driveway; he could see what looked like to be a staggeringly massive mansion about a half a mile away. Matthew was seriously impressed, but surely a writer couldn't afford such a palatial pile? Old money? Certainly something to ask in the interview.

Seriously starting to sweat in the heat, Matthew arrived at the solid, black painted front door with a gargoyle door knocker, playfully fitting into the gothic looking nature of the house. It reminded Matthew of the hotel at Bray which had been used in the sixties to do the Hammer Horror Dracula films. The door opened, and a small woman with long flowing silver hair down past her shoulders smiled and held her hand out for him to shake.

'Hello there, I am Maria, Peter's wife. Welcome to our home,' she said holding the door open for him as he stepped inside. A blast of air conditioning hit him, a blessed relief from the stifling heat. The house that was inherently impressive from the outside was more so when he walked down the marble hallway into the reception room, where Peter van Basel sat, in a massive leather wingback chair, a folded newspaper on his lap and a massive grin on his face.

'Matthew,' he near shouted, placing the paper onto the small table at his side and getting up slowly, a slow wince of pain settling on his face for the briefest of moments. Then it was gone, replaced again by that infectious smile, and all nerves that Matthew was feeling had vanished, and he strode across the room in a couple of paces and shook the elderly gentleman's hand. It was a surprisingly strong handshake, and as the two men's eyes met, Peter chuckled, 'I've still got a bit of strength in me for an old bear! Please, sit down.' He waved his hand to the other chair and Matthew sat, placing his bag between his feet and nodded his head in agreement when Maria asked him if he would like a cold drink of home-made lemonade.

'I have a little present for you, Matthew!' Peter said, walking to the door at the far end of the reception room. 'I found the original manuscript for a story that got me into a hell of a lot of trouble. I assume you're familiar with *Headsoup for the Hole*?'

All of Matthew's Christmases came at once. His body exploded with the sweetest adrenalized joy any human being on the planet could feel. He looked at Peter will puppy dog devotion in his eyes and could only nod dumbly.

Peter's face went from kindly, smiling old man, to a look of utter anger.

'Christ woman, I like this...'

Matthew looked around bemusedly, and his last split-second on earth was spent looking at the keen edge of a hand axe. He noticed a small nick in the otherwise sharp metal, and then it crunched into the top of his head, obliterating frontal lobe and Matthew was instantly quite dead.

Peter came charging across the room as Maria was already on the poor boy, pulling the axe out and letting it drop onto the plush carpeted floor. He went to strike her, but she looked up and hissed and Peter lowered his hand.

'I've not had a bite to eat since the fucking florist three months ago and I'm starving,' Maria said as she stuck her hands into the crevasse that was Matthew's forehead and tugged out a bit of brain which she duly popped into her maw. She bit into it and giggled as a clear liquid escaped from the corner of her mouth and dribbled down her chin. 'Peter, every meal you bring me, means that I won't have to feast on *you*,' she said, looking into Matthew's bag and pulling out the pristine copy of *She Bites*.

'Look Peter, this copy is in even better nick than yours is!' Then she realised she had picked it up with a bloody hand. She grinned evilly.

'I'm going out to the garden to do a spot of digging. I want him gone by the time I get back,' Peter said disgustedly. As he left the room the usual sounds of the axe reminded him that yes, one day it would be his head she'd be nibbling into if her 'tastes' weren't catered to.

By the time he got back from the garden, the body was gone and Maria's silver hair was completely red.

DEAD FOREST AIR

I BOARDED A TRAIN at Munich to take me to Dachau, a town, my battered *Lonely Planet* book told me, was known mainly for the concentration camp and the deaths of between 20,600 to 230,000 prisoners. I later found out that the massive discrepancies in estimates were put down to the trainloads of unregistered prisoners who were offloaded and gassed straight away. There were many, many train loads.

While I was in Germany to know more about the people and its history, I didn't know if I was ready to go and visit a place marking the extermination of thousands of people because they were deemed untermenschen by people who decided life or death with in a heartbeat. It was only during a rather drunken "discussion" with a hairy engineer called Fred, when he implored me to go and to never forget, and to pass on what I had seen so nothing like that could ever happen again. I didn't want to mention Bosnia, Iran, Syria.

So that morning in the Munich Youth Hostel I looked at my *Lonely Planet* and saw that there was a reasonably cheap *gasthaus* in Dachau so I decided to go for it. It wasn't a long journey, I sat in my seat reading *Frankenstein* and eating a cheese sandwich. Though as the train slowly pulled into the station, there was a strange feeling of unease nestling in my stomach. All of those people, packed into those carriages like cattle, cramped, dying of thirst, the cold and not knowing what their fate was going to be. I didn't want to be here. But then that would be too easy. It would be like denying that it ever happened.

I got off of the train.

The guesthouse was small and clean and was owned by Nikole

and Horst Sanders, an elderly couple who loved to go ballroom dancing. They had won several trophies and he delighted in spinning his wife around for a few turns in the living room before crashing into the urn which contained his wife's mother's ashes. We all stared at the mess on the floor. My pidgin German not being up to scratch back then, only caught the tail end of the furiously fast argument where Horst was threatening to vacuum up the remains.

My room was basic but clean, a single bed, washbasin and a small black and white television that took ages to come to life and once it did, the images were faint, ghostly. With my rucksack unpacked, I lay on the bed watching the news and feeling hungry. I slept for an hour, dreamless dozing. When I awoke my hunger was ferocious so I decided to walk into town and see if I could get myself some curried sausage and chips which had become my staple diet in Germany, that and Reisen chews; then hit the pub for a few beers.

Feeling suitably full after an unhealthy mix of currywurst and chips, I stopped in at a small pub. I ordered myself a beer, a Jager-meister and a packet of HB smokes. The barmaid, determining that I spoke English asked me if I would like to pay then or later. When I asked if it was okay if I paid later, she placed a beer mat in front of me and wrote on it what I owed. When I enquired as to what it was, she said that every time I desired a drink I should take my beer mat with me and it would be marked on and then I hand it over when I was done and settle the bill. Nodding my thanks, I put the smokes in my top pocket, downed the Jager and took my beer and sat down at a table and pulled out *Frankenstein*.

I finished my pint and got up to get another, when four girls and two boys walked in. One of the girls smiled at me briefly as she and her friends got their beers and disappeared through a door at the back of the pub. As the barmaid pulled me another Weissbrau, I asked her what was through the back. A pool table, she said.

Grabbing my jacket and book, I wandered up to the door and slowly opened it and peered in. One of the guys was setting up a game. The girl who had smiled at me was seeing which of the pool cues was the shortest.

'Hi, I'm Mark,' I said.

'So Mark, why do you come to Dachau?' Peter asked me, his eyelids half shut, his chin wet with dribble. I had my arm around Hannah and she was kissing my neck, her hand running up and down the inside of my t-shirt. Peter's girlfriend, Liza, was underneath a table, snoring gently.

The others in the group had left ages ago. Now it was just us four in the front bar. The barmaid seemed to be happy serving us at two in the morning. Hannah had taken an instant shine to me, and that was good enough for the others in the group. We were drinking and smoking and at one stage Hannah and I went into the toilet for a few lines of the cocaine that was being passed about in the pool room. There was no language barrier as all could speak excellent English.

'I came to see the concentration camp.'

'Okay, that's a reason, I suppose.'

He looked at me and smiled sadly.

'Time for bed Zebedee,' I said, picking up a Jagermeister and downing it.

'WAS? I mean, what?' Peter enquired.

'Nothing, just a line from a children's television program. The Magic Roundabout'

'Oh, okay the film with Robbie Williams?' I groaned at this, but he seemed not to notice. 'But this is a good idea. Bed. You go back with Hannah to your place? Or you go to hers?'

I grabbed Hannah gently by both shoulders and gently pushed her away from me so I could examine her. Her eyes were heavily glazed and she smiled, trying to stroke my face with affection, but ending up slapping me.

'Does she live far?'

'No, she stays with Liza around the corner. I'm sure she will be happy to have you back.' Hannah kissed me on the nose, closed her eyes and slumped into me.

FUCK.

As soon as I opened my eyes I knew it was a bad idea, tried to close them quickly, but the damage was done.

FUCK.

I pushed back the covers and found that I was still fully clothed, my boots on and mud all over the bed sheets. I looked across the bed and there was Hannah, also fully clothed, her face waxy and white, lipstick smeared across her face.

I got up and collapsed onto a wicker chair, holding my head in my hands. I groggily looked at my watch: nine am.

I wrote a quick note apologising for the sheets, and if she wanted I would meet her for lunch at the pub. I finished the note by saying I had a great time and I would love to see her again. I crept out of her place and ran to the guesthouse, vomiting twice along the way.

Horst was fine with me not making it back, nudging me a few times and whispering about whether she had shaved her armpits or not. I sat at the table, picking at the bread and cheese, drinking sweet tea and just wishing that I were in bed, sleeping the bitch off. I told Horst I would be staying two more nights and he was fine with that but I would have to leave Monday, as the room was booked, but he could find me another place to sleep if I decided to stay in the area. Horst nudged me again when he said this.

After breakfast I went for a long shower and slept for a few hours. Waking at twelve, still blurry, I went to the pub. The same barmaid who had closed up when we left was there again. She passed me a note.

Mark, I have to work this day, but I finish at five. Go and have a look around. We will party later. You also owe me for laundering the sheets. Hannah x.

Grinning, I stuffed the note into my pocket. The barmaid asked if I wanted a beer, and I reacted with mock horror. Later, I said, holding up both hands and retreating.

I wandered around town, taking in the sights and then decided to go to the concentration camp. My brain was still numb from the previous night's festivities so I thought that wandering around the concentration camp wouldn't be as much as a shock to the system as if I went fully alert, brain cells firing with aplomb.

I was, of course, wrong.

The tour was led by a thin, wiry gentleman with a handlebar moustache and ladylike hands. He took us to the place where the showers had once released Zyklon B, a substance that when it was pumped through the showers, turned into a deadly gas from which there was no escape. Dying by this, the Guide said flatly, was the most hideous death known to man.

I looked at the other members of the tour. They were mainly Americans, fat, and fresh off of a tour bus. They took photos. Laughed and really had no comprehension of what had happened here, in this room of slow death.

We were led to another room, where there were meat hooks hanging from the low beams. People were hung from these meat hooks and left there to die, the Guide continued. Some were children. At this the Americans fell silent and stared at each other sheepishly.

My stomach lurched and I thought I was going to throw up. We were then led to where the ovens were; two rust eaten ovens that were sitting one above the other. They were small. Bodies had to be folded in half before they were put in. A massive candle, four foot in height was placed next to the ovens and the Guide said that as soon as a candle was near to going out, a new one would take its place. An eternal memorial.

Outside I could barely breathe. The day had turned grey and grainy. I stared at a mural near the entrance, silently contemplating. The guide sidled up to me and touched my arm gently. 'That mural,' he said, 'is holding up the wall behind it. It's riddled with bullet holes. They lined up the prisoners and shot them. See that at the base of the wall?' I nodded dumbly. 'That made sure that the blood spilled was taken away and drained.'

I stared at him, wondering if he was getting some sick pleasure from telling me all this, but no, he was just passing on the truth. An impassive face, but one so dulled by his job that recounting these horrors had become as normal as breathing.

Had become as normal to him as the killing had become to the Nazis, but that was a thought that was utterly unjust and I felt terrible the moment I had it. I smiled at him weakly, and he left.

The tour finished and I walked slowly away from the concentration camp with the view of going to my bed. It was only two pm so there was still a good while before I met up with Hannah. Then I noticed a path that went up a hill and into the forest. I decided to go for a wander.

I had been walking for about half an hour. I roughly knew the way I had come, I was good with directions and had always managed to keep my bearing, no matter how drunk I often became. The trees had thinned out somewhat by the side of the path, and I thought I would brave it and climb up a tree lined hill to see what was on the other side. Reaching the top, I looked down, the trees were more close together now, soft light filtering through the branches. I took a step, what I thought was a careful one, but slid, and fell down the hill, my jeans streaked with mud. I stood upright at the bottom of the hill, brushed myself down, grinned and took another step and fell again, this time landing in a dip on the forest floor. It was then I realised that there was something amiss with this particular forest. I sat up, cocking my head from side to side. No sign of life. No birds singing in the trees, no animals wandering about. The only noise a whisper of wind coming through the trees. It was deathly silent. I don't think I had ever experienced silence like it. As I pushed myself up, my hand pressed down on something. I picked it up, and looked at it. A wooden heel of a shoe, very old with rusty nails embedded into it. Taking it with me I decided that enough was enough and clambered back up the embankment and walking past the entrance to the camp I caught up with the guide who had finished his shift for the day and was lighting up a very slim, but long cigarette. I told him what I had found.

'Where did you find this?' He enquired. I told him. He told me to follow him back into the camp and to a place he called the map room. As much as I was loathe to go back inside, I followed obediently. In the room, which was rather large and airy, he mused to himself as he traced his finger over a very large map that had been pasted down on a table. His finger seemed to be following a line that cut through the forest and then tapped his finger twice onto the paper. 'I thought so. This heel of a shoe, and the dip in the ground. You found yourself in a mass grave. They took out around two thousand bodies from there in the early fifties.' My spine turned into chilled water. I didn't know if that was the explanation why there was no birdsong, no noise of any kind, but it could be *the* only reason why.

'You've got to be SHITTING me,' I gasped, turning over the wooden heel with my hands.

'No. There is no shitting of you. This is fact. You fell into what was once a mass grave.'

I gave the guide the wooden heel and told him it was only right that it was given to him. He nodded silently and placed it gently on the map. I started to cry. He reached out with his thin ladylike hand and squeezed my shoulder gently.

At five, I was in the pub, still reading *Frankenstein*, but my heart wasn't really in it. Hannah arrived, looking windswept and lovely, followed by Peter and Liza. I ordered the drinks.

'So Mark, you make party with us tonight?' Peter enquired? Hannah took my hand in hers and she smiled at me. 'Not really,' I said. 'It's been a bit of an emotional day. I went to the concentration camp this afternoon, it's drained me.'

Peter nodded sagely. 'I understand, it's a terrible wrench, and a very horrendous place to visit, but you must remember Mark, that life does go on and we like you, and think you are fun and we shall drag you out of this funk and get you to party!'

I had to laugh at this, Peter's enthusiasm was just too infectious.

'Okay,' I said, holding my hands up, palms out, as if in defeat. 'What do you have in store?'

'We'll just make the beer drinking a little bit more interesting. Have you ever done acid, Mark?'

'I was born to do acid, Peter.' I said, downing my pint. 'Show me what you've got.'

Two hours later and everything was going peachy. My head was suitably fucked, I had a gorgeous German girl who wanted to do dirty things to me when we got back to hers, and there was a VW Beetle growing out of a stuffed moose's head.

Coming back with another round of beers on a tray, I had a thought.

'I went for a walk in the forests near the concentration camp today. Shall we go up there for a laugh?' Everyone was thunderstruck. Liza was the first to react. 'Mark, No! This is not a good idea. Those woods, they go on for miles and miles and they are haunted. Full of the dead and you cannot disrespect them in this way. This is not a good idea in the cold light of day, so how would it be when we are all tripping on acid in the dead of night?'

Hannah gripped my arm, she didn't look too please with me. 'Mark, please no. This is an incredibly stupid idea. On this acid, our brains will turn into marshmallows if we went exploring in this way.'

Everyone giggled at the thought of our brains turning into marshmallows. The giggles turned into laughter and the laughter turned into us leaving the pub, going back to Hannah's for torches and booze for a wander up into the woods.

'Whose stupid fucking idea was this to go here in the first place?' I yelled at the trees. The girls were holding onto each other, stroking each other's hair and sobbing. Peter was threatening to do hand to hand combat with me. I looked up at the sky. Full moon and the stars were twinkling, burning, *exploding*. My head was folding in and in and in on itself and I was desperately trying to remember where we came off of the path to see the mass grave. Not knowing where we were going, I led them deeper and deeper into the woods.

'Okay,' I said shining my torch at the girl's faces. They cowered away. 'I will get you out of here, I promise.' I closed my eyes and tried to summon the deep drunk compass. No matter how pissed I get, I'll always find my way home.

But Mark. You're not pissed. You're tripping.

A twig snapped next to me and I spun around, catching Peter in the act of trying to knock me out. The light blinded him. I lashed out, kicked him in the nuts and as he fell onto the ground I ever so gently placed my shoe clad foot on his windpipe. Hannah screamed and dragged me away from him. She slapped me.

'What that fuck do you think you're doing Mark? Violence here? In this place?' I tried to say that Peter went for me first, but she took no notice.

After Peter got his breath back, total clarity came to me. I knew the way home. I pointed my torch to the left, *knowing* that that was the way. Something winked in the torch light.

'What the hell is that?' I asked, shaking the light at it. I took a couple of steps forward and my foot suddenly met with a sharp drop that felt unnatural, almost man made. I pointed my torch downwards.

Peter joined me and shone his torch, as did the girls.

In front of us were around a hundred bodies, naked or dressed in filthy torn rags, pitifully thin, ribcages visible and jutting. They were lying in this dip on the forest floor. As our torches splashed over them, we saw splotches of red, bullet holes, knife wounds, missing flesh, slit throats. They were all dead.

'Fuck this,' Peter yelled, pulling the girls with him. They started to scream, but to my ears it sounded as if they were standing half a mile away from me.

Once gone, I stood there, unable to move, a part of the deathly silence, as from the middle of the mass of dead bodies an arm, a child's arm, broke free and started to feel around for purchase. Putting all thoughts of the acid trip aside, knowing that somehow we had collectively transcended the effects of the drug, I knelt down and begun to clamber over the bodies, knowing if I could just save one, just save...

My torch light winked out.

A loud crack seemed to split the woods in half, then another, another. Screams rent the air around me, high pitched and full of the worst kind of agony. I floundered, tried to push myself up, but my hands could find no purchase. Then a voice barked, full of command and raw power, *Sind sie tot? Sind sie tot?*

I tried to take a shallow breath in, but couldn't. Another burst of gunfire, this time into the pile of bodies I was lying in. It was then I screamed, a full-lunged primal wrench and all of a sudden the bodies and ground beneath me plummeted and my mind stretched, I could *feel* it stretching, and as I was falling I was looking up at a man, in his forties, dressed in full Nazi regalia, holding a machine gun. His hellish grin followed me down as the first sweeps of unconsciousness washed over me.

When I came to the morning was grey and misty. I looked around; everything was leaving slight trails, as if my mind was trying to play catch up with my eyes. Trying to get a bearing on my surroundings, I rolled over and onto my knees and looked for any sign of the local Neo-Nazi scum who were playing *The Game of Reich*. It was then that the horrific images from last night came flooding back, as fresh and as brutal as they were when I was tripping. The drugs had certainly done some damage to my head. I vowed never to drop anything more than an ibuprofen. My stomach lurched and I threw up, a dismal, watery effort.

Once my stomach, and I, had calmed down I lit up a smoke and saw that there were some broken branches hanging off a tree, so decided to head in that direction. Three minutes later, to my amazement I found a very thin path that cut through the woods and after twenty minutes of continual walking, came to a very high chain link fence. Looking through I noticed that I had arrived at the back of the concentration camp. I mouthed a silent thanks to the inner compass for getting me back in one piece (even though my moral compass seemed to have gone to hell) and followed the perimeter of the fence round until I was at the front of the camp. A car drove passed. I stared at it, dazedly. The driver was a young man with shaggy hair and a goatee beard. He gave me the finger and sped off.

I hurried back to the bed and breakfast and let myself in. Horst was taking through some dirty dishes from the dining room to the kitchen and he stopped in surprise when he saw me.

'My god boy, what kind of kinky sex games were *you* playing last night?' I looked down at myself, my clothes were heavy with thick, dried mud.

'It was a bit of a night,' I conceded, and taking off my trainers which were beyond ruined. Thank god I had a pair of good sturdy walking boots as back-up. 'You have a bin I can throw these in?' He nodded and pointed me in the direction of the kitchen.

I showered, put on fresh clothes and wrapped up my filthy ones in a carrier bag and buried them deep in the bottom of my rucksack. I'd take them to a laundry in the next town I went to.

I was taking money out of my wallet when there was a soft knocking at my door. It was Horst, his face was ashen.

'Boy, the Police are here to see you,' he said, opening the door up. Two men, plain clothes, walked into the room.

'Going anywhere?' the first one asked, eyeing the rucksack.

'Yes, of course,' I answered, 'I'm backpacking and I've quite frankly had my fill of Dachau, so I'm off to Chemnitz, see the sights.'

'I'm afraid you won't be able to go anywhere for a while, not until you help us with our enquiries.' His English was crisp, succinct.

'Enquiries, what, those idiots that were running through the woods last night letting off machine guns? You better get that sorted out, it's a fucking blasphemy.' I lit up a cigarette and inhaled the smoke in deeply.

'No, we'd like to ask you questions in relation to the deaths of Peter Muller, Liza Machen and Hannah Brandner. We believe you were the last person to see them alive, so you are, as I am sure you'll understand, of great interest to us.'

THE ROOKERY

H E WAS A QUIET MAN, and had lived with the shards of his divorce with long-suffering stoicism for many years. He had been very careful not to let the world outside the walls of his two bedroom flat see how badly damaged he was, keenly aware of the consequences that could befall him.

From seeing his son every day, to then only having him for a night and a day once a fortnight, was punishment he knew he didn't deserve—but the courts judged otherwise. He had committed no crime, other than the one of marrying the wrong woman. And Lucy, whom he had loved with everything he had, had created a valley of bear traps and dared him to make his way across.

Whenever Roger dropped Sean off, after the precious little time they had together, he would go back to his flat, open up a bottle of whisky and drink as hard as he could. That soulless void would swallow him up until daybreak, when it was ready to spit him out.

The police had come to visit Roger after he informed them of his house move—a visit in accordance of the law, to make sure that the home for the two double barrelled shotguns, a junior single barrelled shotgun for Sean - a 16 bore, one .22 rifle and one .234, plus several hundred rounds of cartridges and bullets was a secure one, and that the gun cabinet they were housed in could not be broken into. The officer who came round was very impressed with the security measures, Roger said that it had been rather easy to create a hidden panel within the wardrobe to put the cabinet in. The cabinet itself was solid steel with a pry-resistant door and three live-locking deadbolts for added security. It was a top of the range cabinet and cost Roger around seven-hundred pounds, but without it he would have never have been allowed to retain his gun license.

Roger was a gamekeeper for the Leader Estate, five miles away from Earlston. It was a longer drive, now he had moved into the bigger town of the area, Galashiels, but that had been the only place where he could rent at short notice. The estate was owned by Gavin Leader; the last in line of the great whisky distillers and at eighty, he was doing his best to be remembered by holding the biggest pheasant shoots in living memory. There were ten pheasant pens each housing around six-hundred birds, covering 1.3 acres of land. Roger was the head gamekeeper but had never been given the luxury of the gamekeeper's cottage – that had been sold to a couple from America who used it as an occasional holiday home. They had bought it ten years before when Gavin had experienced leaner times. Roger's role as head keeper was to make sure that the pens were intact, and that there was no way that predators such as foxes or Goshawk could get in.

He always made sure that he had Sean along with him when it came to release the pheasants from the pen, father and son overseeing their journey to whatever Nature had in store for the birds. After the gates were opened, Roger and Sean would retreat back to the Landrover and watch while the curious birds took their first tentative steps. The next time they would be seen en-masse like this again, would be in the back of the Landrover, after a good days beating and shooting.

Sean, now twelve, seemed to be handling the break-up of his parents remarkably well, he was a bright boy who always had a smile on his face and loved the countryside, and the life that it offered him, with deep passion. He liked nothing better than showing his knowledge of the land to his father, the lad soaked up information like a sponge, and could quickly tell the difference between fox and badger tracks; and he knew which animals had left which spoors. He was a keen shot too; on the days that they went pigeon shooting together he was a calm and considerate companion, not possessed by an itchiness to shoot at everything that flew overhead. Roger had modified the stock of the boy's sixteen bore, cutting it down and adding a thick layer of rubber to minimise the kick the gun gave when it was fired.

Gun safety and maintenance was paramount and Roger drilled it into Sean at every turn. On the day that Roger had first given Sean his shotgun they had driven out to a turnip field. The turnips had been turned, and as they got out and walked across the claggy soil, Roger had picked a stray one up and put it on the top of the thick gate post.

'Now for one of the most important lessons I can ever teach you,' he said, staring at his son intently. 'This turnip, it's about the same size and weight as a human head.' Roger slung the gun case from his shoulder and undid the leather strap and slid out his Baikal over and under shotgun. He broke the gun and slipped in a single cartridge. Closing it, he clicked off the safety guard and held the barrel about five inches away from the turnip, and fired.

Smoke drifted lazily from the barrel as Roger broke the gun and the cartridge ejected out onto the soil.

'It's a mess hey?' he said softly, reaching out and putting his hand on his son's shoulder. You have to be more than careful every time you load a shotgun, never point it at anyone, not even in jest and you will be fine. There's a little ditty you should know about and it goes like this:

> *Never, ever, let your gun*
> *Pointed be at anyone*
> *For all the pheasants ever bred*
> *Will not repay for one man dead*

'You think you'll remember that, son?'

Sean stared at the remains of the turnip that were spread out over a ten metre diameter and nodded silently. There were other pearls of wisdom from his father, one of them being to never carry cartridges on your body while at a shoot. He was told the story of a young boy from Aberdeen, not much older than Sean himself, who had been out beating, helping to flush the pheasants out from the undergrowth towards the waiting shooters at the end of the field. The boy had startled two cocks from the undergrowth, their high pitched cackling filling up the valley and the man at the end of the field raised his gun and shot twice, bringing both birds down. However, a single pellet from the shots strayed and hit the pocket of the young boy's coat, where he had kept a couple of live cartridges and the blast took out his stomach and killed him.

'Please let me have the boy for the Saturday and the Sunday,' Roger begged his ex-wife who was immovable. *No he could not*, Lucy remarked, Sean had a birthday party to go to on Saturday afternoon, so she expected Roger to pick the boy up at around half five that evening.

'But it's the first shoot of the year, and he never misses it, he'll be so disappointed,' Roger stated, his voice becoming flat and monotone. He knew he wouldn't get the boy, she wasn't doing it to punish Sean, she was doing it to punish him.

Well, it doesn't matter what he thinks, he's been invited to a birthday party and getting him to engage with his peers at these type of things is good for him. Jared says so. Lucy sneered, victory tasting delicious in her mouth.

Jared had been their marriage guidance councillor when the cracks first started to appear after the death of their youngest child, Sarah, to meningitis, and who, after the divorce and after Lucy had gained access of Sean, moved in with her. The betrayal was infinite in its continual destruction.

'*Engage with his peers*? He's only twelve for fuck's sake! Okay, well *you* tell him that he can't go,' Roger snarled, slamming down the phone.

*

The shoot finished at four, the Italians who had been invited, but who were paying the privilege of five hundred pounds per brace of birds shot, were very happy with the day. Roger left the job of tying up the braces, one cock and one hen, to the other keepers on his team. There had also been one woodcock shot, and from it, he took the pin feather and attached it to the tweed material of his flat cap. He drove to Lucy's in a hurry but was there at five on the dot, Sean running out of the house with his overnight bag slung over his shoulder. He jumped into the car, a Metro City X and kissed his dad on the cheek. The Landrover didn't belong to Roger; but as Head Keeper it was his to use within the boundaries of the estate.

'So how did the party go then, son?' Roger asked, noticing the boy's slumped shoulders and forlorn look. It was a good sign.

'I hated it, and the present that mum made me give Emily was just embarrassing, everyone laughed at me.'

'What was the present?'

'A packet of underwear.'

'Jesu... what was your mother *thinking?*'

'I don't know dad, she said that all girls need underwear and it's as good a present as any...all I know is that I never want to go to another party like that ever again. Promise me.'

Roger looked deep into his son's eyes. 'I promise.'

'How was the shoot, did they get much?' Sean chirped, eager to change the subject.

That evening after Sean's bag had been dumped at the flat, they went to eat at local carvery; bemoaning the fact that they were no longer allowed to choose how many Yorkshire puddings, stuffing balls and cocktail sausages, but were rationed to one apiece. Father and son agreed it was a rotten state of affairs.

Once Sean was in bed, Roger sat in front of the telly, a glass of Famous Grouse in his left hand, the phone in his right. He so wanted to phone her, to let her let him take over the lad's care for a while, and, to use one of her fancy words, facilitate the next few years of the boy's growth. But her personality had utterly changed – it wasn't just about his drinking, that had admittedly become heavier when they lost Sarah – it was the fact that she had gone for full rights to prevent him seeing Sean at all, and that dirty knowledge always hung over him.

He didn't know what to think, or what to do. He put the phone back in its cradle and wept.

Roger woke Sean up early on the Sunday morning and they had a cooked breakfast and a glass of orange juice. Roger told the boy that they were going to the Rookery to do a spot of shooting, and at this, Sean's face broke into a massive grin, it wasn't often he was allowed to use the .22. Once they were both dressed, and their packed lunches had been made, they got into the car and drove out of town. Fifteen minutes later they were deep into the countryside, using the back roads up through Langshaw, past Mosshouses Farm and through the collection of houses that made up Nether Blainslie. They reached the so-called Top Field, the upper boundary of the estate, opened then closed the gate behind them before driving down the cut lane which snaked its way to the main house and stables where the Landrover was kept.

They put the radio on, which sometimes cut out when they got to Chapel Wood, but this time the signal held strong and they listened to bands that Sean seemed to like a lot and who Roger had no idea of. They chatted about everything that had happened that week and with the shoot. They checked the snares along several of the runs, not finding any foxes, which Roger said was a good thing, the last few months of culling had certainly done its job with helping to deplete the numbers and would in turn, give the next season's pheasants a better chance. They drove back towards the main house, and then cut wildly off to the left, towards the A68, which they crossed and went deep into the hills, towards several clumps of wood at the far reaches of the estate boundary. Here the grass was that little less green, more stony outcrops to test the four -by-four, it was a drive that had to be taken with care, and those stones had taken a Landrover only a few years ago when a group of shooters from Weymouth drove over the ground too fast and rolled it. One of the men had to have his arm amputated at the General Hospital.

Roger parked up and grinned as Sean, who jumped out and ran to the back of the vehicle and opened the door, pulling out the sheathed .22 with care. The gun in its case was almost as tall as he was, coming up just under his shoulder. But when he shot with it, it seemed to look much smaller in his grasp; such was his mastery of the weapon.

They walked towards Blunderstone Rookery, feeling the air temperature drop as they approached the forest that housed the clamour of corvids, their desolate and rasping caws cutting through the burgeoning winter's air. They walked to the other end of the trees, a thin spread of mainly ash and sycamore, away from where the hundreds of birds had their heavy twig nests that bobbed gently as the wind carried them.

Inside the forest it was darker, quieter, and they walked carefully over the fallen branches and carpets of needles which were brown and brittle and made a pleasing scrunch underfoot. There was a coo above them and Roger silently pointed to a pigeon that was on a top branch of a pine about thirty metres away. Sean pointed at the .22 and Roger nodded, pulling a magazine of eight bullets from his pocket and pushing it into the rifle and pulling back the bolt lever, bringing the top bullet from the magazine into the breach. He made sure that the silencer was threaded on safely and that the safety catch was still on and passed the gun to his son, who took it solemnly, and used a low branch from a tree that he was standing next to, to rest it on. He squinted through the scope, raising the barrel up by increments until he was satisfied, then released the safety catch, breathed in and pulled the trigger.

The gun coughed and the pigeon fell through the branches and hit the underground with a quiet thump. As he had been taught, Sean ejected the spent casing, then lowered the barrel towards the ground and put the safety catch back on, before handing the gun back to his father.

'Good lad, now go and bring it back, see how cleanly you caught it,' Roger said, propping the rifle up against the tree.

Sean ran off and was swallowed by the forest.

The wind whipped by Roger as it raced to catch up with the child.

After a minute of scrabbling around, Sean came back with the dead bird clutched in both hands. He presented it to Roger, who saw the deep red hole where the bullet entered in the middle of the bird's chest, an instant kill shot. The thought of the bullet costing more than the bird did entered briefly into his head, but was chased out by the fact that this was a shot and a half. A pearl of blood oozed out from the wound and down the grey plumage of the birds chest and rolled to a stop.

'Would you like to come and live with me Sean?' Roger asked, opening up the bird's wing to its full span. 'I've been thinking that I could use my savings to get a better lawyer and I could go for full access and...'

'Dad, I can't,' Sean said quickly. 'I would have to move school and I would lose my friends and it's hard enough as it is. As much as Mum is a pain, I couldn't leave her. Not just yet.'

'Oh,' was all Roger could say. He left the wing go and it snapped back against the body.

Roger frowned at the bead of blood, prodded at it with his finger then leant down and placed the bird on the ground. As he straightened his back up, a bolt of bad electricity ran through him, his throat constricted and his scrotum shrivelled up into his stomach.

'Son,' Roger croaked, pointing ahead into the darkness of the forest. 'Is that a deer? Turn around very, very slowly and tell me if you can see that deer hiding in the trees.'

Sean's face beamed, deer were his favourite animal. He did as he was told, and he peered into the trees as hard as he could.

'I don't see anything dad,' he whispered.

'Just...keep...on...looking,' Roger said, taking and lifting the rifle to his shoulder, tears running down his face. Roger felt something snap deep inside his head as he released the safety, like an old shoelace pulled too quickly.

He fired, the silencer coughed once, like an old man clearing his throat in the library. Sean fell over, face first, into the brittle twigs and needles that covered the forest floor. The gun fell free from his shoulder, and the butt swung out, though his leading hand held the stock firm.

Roger looked around wildly; darkness was attacking him from all sides, a suffocating smog dulling his reflexes, the hand not holding the rifle scrabbling at his throat, pressing his windpipe in as if that would open it up. He gulped for air, his vision swimming in and out like low tide. The tops of the trees danced in the wind far above him. He felt like he had come up from the bottom of the earth itself.

Sean.

Roger kneeled down by him and blinked furiously when he turned his son over. The child's glazed eyes had rolled back into their sockets. A stream of blood that seemed to glow bright in the midst of the woods gloam poured from the exit hole, the size of a Clementine in the middle of Sean's forehead, running down the side of his nose, then down his cheek and neck.

Roger fell back and started to scream. But it was fake; screaming when nobody was there to hear it. A rook flew from the tops of the trees and landed on top of the boy's shoulder. Small, beady white eyes regarded the father coldly, then it turned its head and the bone white beak burrowed into the hole in the boy's forehead. It pulled something from the killing wound and ate it and then cackled victoriously, flapping its wings, the bone white beak now stained heavily with Sean's blood.

Roger finally seemed to realise what was going on. 'Leave him!' Roger groaned, raising the rifle and looking through the scope. The barrel wobbled around drunkenly, but then he had it, right between the eyes. His finger pulled the trigger but nothing happened, then he remembered the safety catch. Habit. The rook left the boy and seemed to be coming at Roger, covering the ground between them very fast. In those few seconds its form seemed to shift, from rook to a shroud of billowing smoke, decaying face grinning with pleasure, ancient earthy fingers reaching for him, then back to its original form. The safety clicked off and Roger fired, hitting the thing right between the eyes, the air was sucked out of the woods, then breezed back through the trees, ruffling the bits of Sean's hair that remained unmatted by his blood and the bird hit the floor.

The police found the bodies at Blunderstone Rookery by lunch the next day, Roger was sitting against a twisted and skeletal elm tree, the barrel of the rifle in his mouth and the back of his head plastered onto the ancient bark. The police had already visited the flat after Lucy informed them of their history and there they found the suicide note. It was Gavin who phoned the police when he had heard a report on the news about the missing pair and told them that Roger's car was still parked next to the stables. In it, they found two packed lunches, the ends of the cut ham and cheese sandwiches curling.

As the remains were removed carefully from the scene, the rooks flew above them, twisting in the winter wind, corvids communicating with their throaty caws.

It sounded like laughter.

PRIM SUSPECT

A MIE HIRD SAT AT HER DESK in the corner of her writing space, turned on the word processor and waited for it to load up. She had been walking in the park earlier that morning when an idea for a story struck her so hard she didn't notice a dog barrel towards her, chasing a ball thrown by its owner. The dog knocked her clean onto her behind, but she wasn't all that bothered.

She had hurried back home to start on the story straight away, but a message on the machine stopped her. It was from Primrose Hildebrand, local snoop who never took no for an answer. Not from *anybody*.

'Amie,' Primrose's tinny voice yapped from the large answer-phone, 'I need you to bake some cakes for the Circle Ladies meet this Sunday. Normally Jean Buddock would be doing the honours but she's in the hospital getting her womanly hope removed. Now we want light and airy, nothing that would sink a ship, two dozen, and I want you to deliver them to me tomorrow afternoon, which is of course Saturday. I know how you writers lose track of time when there is quite fran—'

Primrose's time on the answerphone had ended and Amie thought with a grin that made the wrinkles round her eyes more pronounced, that she would hate that, oh yes indeed. She was surprised that Primrose hadn't phoned again to either finish off the message or leave a dose of vitriol for the answerphone's discour-tesy. Though there would be time enough for that when Amie delivered the cakes.

So Amie had baked not one, but two batches and only when they were out on the window ledge, cooling down, did she decide that it was time to get her idea down quickly before it dulled.

Whilst baking, she had gone over and over it in her mind and it was really rather good.

The green of the monitor glowed at her and she opened up a new document and started to write.

It wasn't every day that Samantha came up with a good idea for a story, but when she did, she liked to go to the lakehouse and sit in the soft glow of the summer evening with her writer's pad and pencil to shape out plots, characters; even try to have some kind of ending to aim for. Her output only amounted to three or four short stories a year, mostly sold to the one magazine in the UK that covered her style of writing. If she was lucky, she might sell one to an anthology which catered to fans of horror and the supernatural. To look at her, Samantha appeared to be your normal, everyday housewife —and she was. She worked as a social worker, told nobody about her writing and had it published under a man's name—which she asked her cousin Craig if she could use; it was good for the payments to go to him as well and she made sure that each Christmas, Craig was looked after with a bottle or two of Glenfiddich.

After a few good hours scribbling away, during which time she'd come indoors as it became too dark to work, she picked up the telephone and held it to her ear. She was about to dial her home number where, Frank, her husband would no doubt be wondering where she was and where his dinner had got to.

Samantha's face scrunched with confusion; there were two people on the line having a heated conversation. She held the phone tighter to her ear, trying not to make a sound, lest they heard her overhearing.

"I'm telling you, we have to dispose of her, cut her up into hundreds of pieces and feed her to whatever pig farms there are in the area," *the first voice said, his voice high and nasal, his accent flat and untraceable.*

"It's too much hassle; do you really want to be spending a whole day sawing her head, arms and legs off? You got the spine to get through, ribs to snap off and don't forget, she might be a bloodless bitch, but that doesn't mean she won't have blood in her. And there's the clean-up afterwards, bleaching everything down—because if you were to get busted, the cops have these new lights that bring up traces of blood on everything. One of the guys back in jail was talking about it."

The second voice was gruff and with a strong Irish brogue. Samantha listened to the conversation between the two men with dawning horror. She tried to keep her breathing to a minimum, but her heart started to trip out, get faster and faster, the room started to swim...

"Hey, who's that on the line," *the Irishman shouted.* "Who the fuck is this?"

Samantha fell to the floor, taking the phone with her, pulling the lead out of its socket. A dead tone, then a high pitched pipping sound.

Amie sat back in her chair looking over her work. Satisfied, she ran her hands through her greying blonde hair and got up, the twinge in her back making her wince. It was the only price she had to pay for her writing, but it was a tough one. She found that she could only write at her desk, impossible to do when sitting slumped down on her sofa. She went to the fridge, brought out a decent bottle of white and opened it, pouring herself a tall glass and drank it in near one gulp. Gasping with delight she poured herself another, taking this one much more slowly—the buzz had already started around her temples, a few more sips and she would feel light as a feather. To make sure that her back wouldn't bother her anymore for that evening, she went to the bathroom, opened up the cabinet and pulled out a bottle of tablets that she had procured from Dr. Probe during an extremely excruciating period. It bore the legend DO NOT TAKE WITH ALCOHOL. She took two, and swallowed them with another swig.

Going back to the word processor, she took a new disc from its box, put it into the drive and saved the story. She wondered if she should do a little bit more, but decided that the buzz was too good to waste on writing. Amie wondered if it was time for *Blockbusters* to come on. Even though he was getting on a bit, Bob Holness was a dish.

She came to in the small hours of the morning. Samantha cried out, thinking that the two men were in the room with her, the conversation coming back to her in gruesome snatches.

"Feed her to whatever pig farms are in the area."

"Sawing her head, arms and legs off."

"Ribs to snap off."

Samantha got up slowly, feeling her way up the telephone table and once upright, took two delicate steps before she came to the wall. Sliding her hand across it, her fingers touched the light switch and she stabbed at it frantically, on her third attempt the room was suffused with the harsh glare of a one-hundred watt bulb. She walked to her sofa and collapsed onto it as the tears began, tears of confusion and self-pity: of being alone in a place miles away from home—no matter that it belonged to her father. The lake house seemed alien, the years of happy memories of summer holidays here wiped from the face of the earth with the overheard snatch of a sick phone call.

Looking at the phone again she wondered if she should plug it back into the wall. But what if they were there, on the line, waiting for her? What if they had some kind of trace so that they knew where she had been? She gathered that she'd been out of it for a while, so what if they were already on their way to her?

Samantha screamed involuntarily as she heard a car pull up to the gate at the top of the lakehouse, tyres scrunching on the gravel. The handbreak being pulled. The juddering of the engine as it was switched off. She ran to the light switch and flipped it off before running through to the kitchen, banging her knee on the coffee table on the way. Unmindful of the bright flare of pain that ran up her body, she went to the drawers and fumbled through them until she pulled out a kitchen knife, its handle worn with years of use. The blade was still keen and honed though. Her hand trembled as she held the knife in front of her. She padded silently to the front door of the house and crouched at the foot of the stairs, a cat ready to pounce. The knife twitched ready to sink into the warm flesh of any attacker who wanted to rape and then strangle her to death with her own tights.

The door opened and she screamed, lunging forward to bring down the knife in the style of old mother Bates in Psycho. The attacker fell under the first blow and raised his hand to his neck and gargled, "Sama..."

Her blood turned to ice. She looked for the light switch and once she had found it, stared at her husband Frank, blood jetting from his neck. She screamed and fell to him, telling him that she thought he was an attacker. She pulled the knife out and he groaned, his eyes rolling back into their sockets, blood splashing up and then dribbling down the walls.

Even though she had a bitch of a hangover the writing was coming along well, Amie thought. She hadn't plotted for Frank to be killed so early on, and especially not by his own wife; it threw the story into utter disarray and she would have to completely rewrite, making all of her notes moot save for one or two character snippets. Amie took another sip of Alka-Seltzer imbibed water and rubbed her forehead gently. She was mindful of the time and the drive she had to take down to Primrose's to deliver the cakes. After phoning her mother and having to go through the excruciating task of dissecting the breakdown of her latest relationship, (he was a teacher, it had lasted six months and the sex was just too much for her back to take—although she would never tell her mother *that*), there would just be enough time to go to the chemists, pick up some bits and pieces then go and see Primrose.

'Please come in,' Primrose said, opening the door wide enough for Amie to walk through sideways and no more. 'You parked your car in the bandstand car park and walked up I hope? It's not that I mind people knowing that you're here of course; it's just that I don't want Susan Brook bothering me today. If she comes to the door I can just pretend that I'm not in.' Primrose looked shifty, almost guilty.

'I don't think Susan will be bothering you Primrose, didn't you hear that her husband Nigel died?' Amie said, sitting down on the chair in the kitchen to which she had been offered.

'Oh, yes of course, of course she wouldn't bother bothering me, she's in mourning, of course,' Primrose vaguely said and went to her range, took the stainless steel kettle from it, went to the sink and filled it up with water. 'So, how's your horror writing coming along?' she asked, walking back to the range and lighting up one of the hobs with a large match stick shaped lighter. The gas caught and "whoomped" slightly. Primrose put the kettle on over the flame and walked back to the kitchen table, her heavy diamond engagement ring twinkling brightly as the sunlight flooding through the windows caught it.

'The writing is coming along fine thanks,' Amie answered, still puzzled by the fact that she had told Primrose about this in the first place. The woman, in her estimation, looked like she couldn't keep a confidence of any sort, nevertheless Amie had gone ahead and told her about her dabbles into writing macabre fiction. Being a writer was okay, you could say that to anyone and get away with it, but to say that you were an author who wrote horror fiction, well that was another thing entirely. Primrose had seemed utterly delighted and promised that she wouldn't tell a soul, a promise she seemed to be keeping. In fact, apart from Primrose's barbed comments and rather acerbic manner, the two women got along fine and Amie actually liked her. She didn't think that her feelings would be returned and would have been surprised to find out that Primrose actually took some stock in what the younger woman said, even though she despised her relative youth and good looks.

When Primrose first met Amie and asked her what she did—she had told her the truth, that her job was as an editor for a small publishing company, she worked from home and had as many manuscripts sent to her as was possible. It was during this time that Amie spotted a Shirley Jackson novel placed neatly next to the bread bin. A leather bookmark revealed that Primrose was more than halfway through.

'I didn't take you for a reader of horror stories, Primrose,' she remarked. Opening it up she saw that it was a first edition, and flatsigned by Jackson herself.

'There's a lot you don't know about me,' Primrose answered dryly. 'Why do you enquire?'

So Amie had told her and promised to bring with her the next time she visited, a copy of her first, and so far only, collection, *The Quiet Carriage and Other Stories*.

And so it began.

Now the two ladies were eating cake and chattering about a "delicious little scandal", as Primrose liked to call it. A rough 'un, straight out of prison who would never lose his penchant for trouble, Vinny Mason, was accused of more than being caught halfway up a tree with a pair of binoculars trained on the window of his ex-French school teacher Adrienne Devline. Seemingly he had already impregnated several of Effingham-on-the-Stour's female populace, the most jaw-dropping of which, was Marie Ludlam, the dentist's wife.

To be honest Amie found the conversation a little distasteful, but Primrose really did seem to get off on the gossip and it was a little infectious.

Amie knew that once Primrose had been married to a gentleman called Ralph, who had died in the factory that he had managed. Primrose had gotten filthily rich from the money he left her. After his death though she didn't venture outside for at least twenty years, deep in mourning and, Amie supposed, it was this self imposed exile that now made her eager to talk and probe and gossip.

'I just need to go to the toilet; will you be okay as you are dear?' Primrose asked, getting up and smoothing down her skirt.

'Yes of course, I'm not planning on doing any writing today. Call it a day off!'

Primrose nodded and disappeared out from the room. Amie looked around the kitchen-dining room, it was tastefully decorated, subtle Victorian that thankfully hadn't been destroyed by the late fifties, early sixties habit of plastering everything with hideous faux wooden units. Her eyes rested on a finely carved mahogany writing dresser at the farthest end of the dining room. On it was a very large looking ledger, gloriously bound in leather. Getting up and pushing the chair back so the feet wouldn't squeak on the stone flags, Amie padded across to the book to see what was in it. *You never know where the inspiration for the next book will come from*, she told herself.

Opening it carefully, she was confronted by the smallest hand-writing she had ever seen in her life. The person who had done this must have used a magnifying glass and have had a severe amount of time on their hands.

Amie squinted and made out the following paragraph.

Blackspur, Jean (Moor House, Effing-ham)—stole several bottles of champagne from the local supermarket and gave them to a young girl (Edwards, Stephanie—16, The Close, Effingham) and the two walked off in the direction of the park. Following them and keeping a discreet distance I watched them perform several sexual acts on each other. I collected the empty bottles and both pairs of underwear that had been left behind, as evidence.

Confused, Amie scanned her fingers down some more writing

then moved onto the next page.

> Williams, Ronald (#69 Little Hams, Effingham) —stole prolifically from his fellow teachers at Effingham High School, was found out by P.E. teacher Elspeth McBeth but was blackmailed into keeping her silence (see McBeth, Elspeth). Discovered on following Elspeth and husband back home after drunken night as she confessed all.

On the entries went, page after page. There must have been hundreds. Amie heard movement from upstairs and closed the book hurriedly and sat back down at the table. Primrose came down the stairs, they only squeaked a few times, if Amie hadn't been on such a hair-trigger she would have been caught poring through the book.

Was she in it?

The thought was awful, intrusive and turned her insides into porridge. Amie wanted to just get up and flee the house, never have to speak to the mad old bag again. Did she have anything on her? What could Primrose possibly know?

'I'll need to go to the shops, I've ran out of Fleur de Lise Miyayakka moisturiser and some other bathroom accessories,' Primrose said brightly, coming back into the room. Amie gave a small token of thanks to the Gods that Primrose didn't look over at the book, hadn't acknowledged its existence.

'Would you like a lift in, Prim?'

'Yes, that would be lovely of you and there'd be no need for you to wait for me. I shall phone a taxi to take me back.' Primrose said, swiping at a fly that was buzzing around them both. 'Shall we go?'

After Amie dropped Primrose off she went to the local village store, settled her milk and newspaper bill for that week and bought two bottles of red wine and half a bottle of Smirnoff. She couldn't get to the house quick enough; as soon as she was through the door the top had come off the first bottle of red and she was drinking deeply, not caring that she needed a glass. *The woman was a fucking monster!* was all that Amie had in her head. What kind of malaise had driven the elderly woman to so obsessively keep secrets on everyone in town?

Collapsing onto the sofa, Amie took another swig and tried to think. What could Primrose possibly have on her, if anything? She had kept the private stuff down to a minimum really, had been vague when it came to talk about her family; or what was left of her family, it had become really messy and splintered after her father had died and that fight that broke out at his funeral, but Primrose would never have found that out. It had been a different time.

'Oh fuck this,' Amie said aloud, struggling up from her nest and walking through to the bathroom. She went to the cabinet on the wall, opened it up and took out her infamous "DO NOT TAKE WITH ALCOHOL" pills. She popped two in her mouth and chased them back with another generous swig. She wanted the day to be over with as quickly as possible.

'Amiiiiiiiiiie. Aaaaaaaaammmmmmmiiiiiiieeeeeeeeee,' a voice whispered to her through the funk of her self-medicated unconsciousness.

'Waaaaaaaa?' She opened her eyes, a hammer of pain crashed behind them. She flopped onto her back, breathing heavily, her right hand pressing down onto her forehead.

'Heeeelllllllpp meeeee Aaaaaamiiiiiiieeeeeeeeeeeeeee!' the voice said. It was high pitched, coupled with a harsh rasping noise, like someone pumping air into a torn football.

Amie groaned once, a prolonged effort and then reached across for the lamp switch. Her hand fumbled a few times before she found it, but then she made contact and the black plastic switch clunked and the room was flooded with light.

That hammer of pain turned into an earthquake of one. She gasped, unable to open her eyes but knowing that she must, that there was something in the room with her. Her eyelids parted, a flood of harsh, unrelenting light assaulted her vision (even though the lamp was home to a lowly 40 watt bulb) but through the pain and the tears, she made out the figure of a man, bleeding profusely, lying next to the bed.

Any thoughts of a hangover vanished in a split second. Amie was alert and threw herself out from under the duvet. The man groaned as she accidently kneed him in the crotch as she bent down to tend to him.

He was in his mid-forties with a kind face that was now smeared with blood. His dark hair was starting to thin, his widow's peak pronounced; to her mind's eye he looked like a more sympathetic John Cazale. Then the alarm bells started to ring and Amie felt her grasp on reality slip several degrees towards bedlam.

Her bedroom door was shut. There was no blood trail, or indeed any blood on the door. It was like the victim had just appeared.

'We need to deal with Primrose, Amie,' the man said, sitting up, the wheezing rasp in his voice still pronounced but any thoughts that the man needed help, apart from seemingly bleeding to death, was out of the window as he started to smile benignly.

'My god, who *are* you?' she nearly screamed. But then it clicked into place, recognition, and the relief flooded over her panicked synapses, took her to her cave of calm.

It was Frank. Fictional Frank. Frank who was stabbed in the neck out by the lakehouse.

Amie passed out, her head hitting the blood-soaked patch of carpet. Frank grinned, patted her shoulder gently and waited for her to come to.

Her forehead felt tacky. Amie touched it gingerly and then looked at her finger. Bloody.

'It's not yours,' Frank said. He was sitting on the chair by the dresser. He had stopped bleeding now; he was probably talking to her with no blood left in him, Amie thought. She almost passed out again.

'There girl, steady as she goes,' Frank said. He was beside her now, grabbing hold of her arm, steadying her. How did he get to her so quickly? His accent seemed neutral, but she knew there was an undercurrent of Brummie in there somewhere. Looking at him she saw that he had very intense, deep brown eyes. Those eyes had wooed Samantha, those eyes had bulged with confusion as his wife plunged a wickedly sharp butchers' knife into his neck.

'Amie, let's be honest, I'm only here because you are having a psychotic breakdown and hallucinations are manifesting because you are hitting the pills and the booze a little too heavily. But don't be too hard on yourself and whatever you do, don't stop taking them. I'm here to help you get rid of Primrose—she has something devastating on you, something she's found out from your old life...'

Amie felt like heart had stopped beating mid-beat. Her body tensed up, turned to concrete. Her mind flashed back to those bad old days, but there was no way that Primrose could ever have found out, she had covered her tracks too well.

'But don't worry,' Frank continued. He coughed and a glut of blood flew out of his mouth and landed on her lap. 'Sorry about that,' he grimaced. 'We'll be able to get rid of her, but first of all you have to break into her house and find out exactly what she has on you, and only then can you proceed. Also... and this may sound strange, but you need to keep writing. Even though you've killed me,' he smiled forgivingly, 'you need to continue with this or I'll lose the power to communicate with you, by proxy.'

'I can't do any more writing,' Amie pleaded—I need to pack up and leave, need to just vanish. I can do it; I've got the money to start over again. I can spend the rest of my life tending to my plants in a lovely cottage garden. I can...'

'...let that despicable cow ruin your life and everybody else's in that book,' Frank finished flatly. 'Firstly, you have to find out if she is working alone, there is a slim possibility that she has someone else under her charge, but I don't think so. Still, better to be safe than sorry.'

'You mean I should follow her?' Amie asked incredulously, wishing beyond hope that the bank would open so she could withdraw all of her savings and start her life on the run.

'Follow her, make sure she isn't colluding with anyone, and when you are sure, wait until she goes somewhere, preferably for the weekend and stage a break-in and see what's in the book. Take the book if you must, do you think that she'd have made a copy? See what dirt she has on you, then when the dust dies down from the break-in, go and pay her a little visit and push her down the stairs. You'll have the book, which you'll be able to dispose of, and the person who you thought of as your *friend* will be rotting peacefully in the cemetery, forever a silent keeper of your biggest secrets.' Frank looked at her. He seemed pleased with himself.

Her hands were surprisingly shake-free. Her mind though, was a shivering wreck, pushed to the brink of insanity. The only thing that was stopping Samantha from tipping over was the fact that she couldn't go to jail if she just told the police what had happened. They would believe her, of course they would. Why wouldn't they?

So why hadn't *she phoned the police?*

Because in her heart of hearts she knew the truth. As soon as Samantha told the police that her husband was dead, she would wait a little while for the blue lights, those twisted and fractured beams coming steadily towards her as they made their way through the trees to the drive at the top of the lakehouse. They would get out of their cars, the ambulance would come in behind, they would approach her, surveying the developing scene. And Samantha would let them in, pulling back the door so they could see him, her dear, dead husband, the carpet

103

underneath him sodden with his blood; when it came for the time to remove the carpet the police would struggle with trying to take it for evidence.

She would cry, and she would mean every tear, but would the police believe her? One kindly, but hard looking detective would sit her down on the sofa, making slight gestures of commiseration and sympathy as he tried to look deep into her soul with his dead, shark eyes, to seek the slightest whisper of a lie.

No! thought Samantha, they would arrest her. She didn't stand a chance. She would spend the rest of her days at the merciless graspings of the multitudes of unwashed jail lesbians that lived in those places.

Samantha looked down at her dead husband, and her mind wandered back to the time he had first approached her in The Swan, a pub she had only gone into three times before, with a lad who turned out to be one of the most accident prone men in Blackwall. She had kindly let him down—well, as kind as letting someone down could be—and decided the day after, a Friday, to go out with some friends and to hell with the consequences. If there was to be a hangover that would split her temples the following day, then so be it. Herself, Tracey and Linda had done the rounds of the four pubs in town and thought it would be a giggle to see if Accident Prone was in there drowning his sorrows. He wasn't, but Frank was; easy going and relaxed, drinking with his mates at the bar, smoking home rolled cigarettes, one eye closed shut as to fend off the smoke that drifted lazily up into the air before it was sucked in by an occasionally working air conditioner.

After the girls had decided which blokes they would make a play for, Samantha had breezed up to Frank, smiling as he stepped back to let her into his space at the bar.

"Will you buy a lady a pint?" *she asked.*

"Yes, of course," *he replied, putting his hand into his pocket for his last ten pound note. Little did he realise that this woman, who loved him with all that her heart could give, would end up snuff—*

'I'm just not feeling this whatsoever,' Amie said, saving what she had written so far. Once that was done, she switched off the word processor and then downed the glass of Chablis that was next to the monitor.

'You're doing very well given the circumstances,' Frank said. Truth be told he was staring at Amie with something akin to awe in his eyes, he was only really beginning to realise the magnitude of what was happening and what he was. He had known nothing of his past; apart from the fact that he was suffering from a case of the terminals and that a woman who purported to be his wife had killed him. The fact that he knew everything about Amie's life, and Primrose and the journal quantified the strangeness of it all. But then he reminded himself that he was only a person in Amie's deep -seated psychosis. as a person he didn't really exist and that thought slowed his wheels for a while.

But it *was* odd. As soon as Amie started writing those words about the first time he and Samantha met, he could smell the bar, years of spilled beer on the carpets, could close his eyes and visualise the yellow, nicotine-heavy wallpaper. He had a memory. Amie had created it for him.

'Maybe I could leave an anonymous tip-off with the police,' Amie mused out loud. 'They don't need to know who it is that's giving them the tip-off, and I'm sure that they'd be interested, I'm sure that there would be some kind of law against doing what she's doing,' Amie descended into rapid babbling. She stalked through to the kitchen and came back, moments later, with a large glass of pinot, which she duly began to demolish. Frank was lounging on a beanbag. He looked remarkably comfortable.

'So, to stay here in this quaint little town, where old hens like to dominate the lesser chicks with fear and treachery, I have to step forward and chop the head Hen's head off?'

Frank nodded and reached out, the seat rustled as he got to his feet. He placed his hand on Amie's shoulder. The hand looked smooth, as smooth as marble, no trace of lines or age. Amie felt sick.

'You'll be fine. Trust me.'

Amie decided that the best course of action was to break into Primrose's house the next time she learned that the old bag was to leave Effingham. It wasn't a normal occurrence—Primrose hardly ever strayed away from the village—but there was the odd occasion and she would always tell Amie where she was going. She would give the reason that it was always good to tell *someone*, just in case she never came back. In between times Amie decided that she would try and cut down on the pills and the booze, for no other reason than to get rid of Frank, who was making himself a little too much at home.

Saturday was spent trying to write, but mainly looking out into space, uninspired, lethargic, a part of her saying how lovely it would be to have a glass or two of the nice wine that she had acquired from a London auction attended the year before. Frank said that he would be in the attic if she needed to talk, he said that the effects of being dead and imaginary were starting to get to him and he needed to 'try and come to terms with the existential conundrum that he found himself in.'

Three hot cups of tea later and Amie had managed to get down two hundred words. The phone rang.

'Hello?'

'Amie? Is that you Amie? It's Primrose speaking. You've done a vanishing act on me girl, whatever's the matter?'

Amie's face started to burn, she flushed red. Instantly Frank was at her side, staring at her intensely.

'Oh, hello Primrose, thanks for calling, yes, I know I haven't really got in touch recently, I've been rather poorly...you know how it is.'

'No, not really,' Primrose said curtly. 'I'm never ill.'

There was a slight pause between the two women before Primrose spoke again.

'I was wondering if you'd be able to help me out on Tuesday. I foolishly said that I would do the cake duties for Wednesday's Circle Meet, but forgot that I had overbooked—there is a Survivors of Cancer meeting the same day but at a different venue. I'm sorry to ask, but would you give up your morning to help? Be lovely to have a catch-up.'

The word 'catch-up' sent Amie's stomach into freefall but she agreed that she would come over and bring her set of scales as Primrose only had the one. Once she had hung up the phone, she got up wordlessly, went into the kitchen, grabbed the bottle of red that was there and finished it off in under twenty minutes.

'Will you do it then?' Frank asked, leaning against the fridge. Amie was sitting at the kitchen table, her eyes glassy.

'Oh, would you just get to *fuck!*' Amie said, throwing the empty glass, it hitting the shrivelled and grey wound on his neck. It was weird the way he looked. He hadn't decomposed like the bloke in the film *American Werewolf in London*, but then neither had his wounds healed. He looked paler and a bit thinner, but if it wasn't for the wound, you would never have thought him dead. Wrap him up in a scarf and send him out shopping. If only he could be seen by others though...

Frank winced. Then rearranged the colourful magnetic letters on the fridge to read 'just do it'. He casually asked to see what she had written, but she shook her head, *no*. He sloped back towards the attic.

Amie and Primrose stood next to each other at the breakfast bar, both with mixing bowls under one arm and wooden spoons in the other. Frank was in the house somewhere, rummaging. Primrose, of course, couldn't see him, and didn't seem to notice that Amie was one step away from jumping out into the abyss. Frank Sinatra was playing on the radio in the background and it was a pleasant day. Occasionally Amie caught a glimpse of her fictional corpse miming to the words when he poked his head in and waved. He was trying to be encouraging. A nicer day for a killing would not be found in this little corner of the world. Amie decided that by the end of the day's cake-baking Primrose's toes would be turning up in her little heeled velvet slippers.

The journal, last spied on the ornately carved mahogany dresser, was nowhere to be seen, hidden out of sight. It was too much to ask that it be left out, Primrose had probably forgotten all about it the last time Amie had visited. Had Prim realised afterwards that she could have had a chance to read it? Did Primrose know? Had Primrose invited her here to do her in? Fear flooded her body. She stopped mixing and put the bowl down on the counter to steady herself.

'What's wrong, my dear?' Primrose asked, genuine concern etched on her face. If she was hiding a revenge attack, she was doing a better job of masking her features than Amie could ever hope to achieve. Indeed, her facade was starting to crumble around her.

'I'll be fine, I don't know what's wrong with me at the moment,' Amie said, inhaling sharply as Frank came right up behind Primrose and started to make slashing motions and nod his head appreciatively.

'You sit over there,' Primrose said, leading her to a chair next to the dresser, 'and I'll go upstairs to the bathroom and find a wonderful effervescent powder that Doctor Probe gave me a few months ago when I was feeling a bit under the weather. It'll fix you right up.'

'Thought you said you were never ill,' Amie tried to joke.

'Don't be a smartypants,' Primrose reproached coldly before disappearing out of the room.

As soon as she was gone, Frank told her that the book was in the top right drawer. Amie reached over and pulled the handle, it was unlocked and the drawer slid out smoothly. The ledger was there, also a small stack of sympathy cards and a blood red fountain pen. Lifting the book out, she laid it on the dresser, opened the cover and frantically started to go through the pages until she came to 'H'. She scanned through the names, *Hambs, Hemberton, Hillaby... Holcombe*. There was no entry for Hird. She turned frantically to Frank who had by now retreated to the bay window. He shrugged helplessly.

'I thought you said she knew?'

So startled by this non-revelation, Amie failed to hear Primrose come into the room.

'I've found one of Doctor Probe's magical powders, a little of this and you'll be as right as—' Primrose stopped and looked from the ledger to Amie and back to the ledger again.

'Well this certainly puts a spin on the day,' Primrose said, walking to the counter and putting the sachet of powder on the marble top, before going to one of the cupboards and taking out a slim glass. She went to the sink and let the cold water run for a while then jutted the glass in and filled it up to the top.

'Does anyone else know about the book?' Primrose asked, opening up the sachet and dumping the contents into the glass. She handed it to Amie who shook her head, no. Sighing, Primrose took it to the sink and tipped it, washed the glass up and dried it with a tea towel that had a duck-billed platypus printed on it.

'Of course, I knew that you had looked at it, there was a little tiny smudge of chocolate from the cake we had when you came around. I wash my hands thoroughly before I handle the book, so I knew that it wasn't me. Then with you being so out of sorts afterwards, it confirmed to me that you had read the book. And you spent all that time stewing over it, wondering if you were in it?'

'Did you finish the Shirley Jackson book?' Amie asked, trying to distract her so she could make her move and take Primrose out.

'I found it all a bit lacking really. She does so try to make a mountain out of a molehill. I think that...'

Amie rushed at her, aiming to barge into her with her shoulder and knock her over. Primrose, as neat as you please, stepped to her left, and grasped a small, metal, meat hammer that was in the drying rack. For an old lady she was lightning quick, and smacked the hammer into the side of Amie's head before the younger woman crashed into her. Amie went down silently, but hard. Primrose brought the hammer down again, for luck.

'Frannngggggk, Frannngggk. Fuggginnnng killll the bitttggcchhh, Frannnggkkk,' Amie mumbled, coming to. The left side of her face felt broken, *was* broken. She tried to move, but she was now sitting down, her hands tied to the back of the kitchen chair. Amie couldn't believe that Primrose had lifted her up and sat her on the chair, but then again, she would never have thought that Primrose could have cold-cocked her so easily.

'Frank? Who's Frank?' Primrose asked, taking a pair of Marigold gloves from one of the drawers next to the sink and putting them on. 'Is he the dirty little secret you managed to hide from me? Am I going to have to sort him out too?'

'Frangggkkkkkkkkkkkkkkkkk!' Amie tried to scream, but then she began to choke. She coughed deeply and spat out three teeth. They spattered onto the linoleum flooring of the kitchen.

Frank was standing just in front of Primrose. He wasn't animated or delighted by the old lady's presence any more. He looked sad, deflated and slightly bewildered by how proceedings had turned out. He tried to speak, but no sound came out. Instead, a jumble of letters, thousands of tiny letters, all in the Times New Roman font, tumbled out of his mouth, hit the floor and turned to dust. Frank's face went from bewildered to alarmed.

Amie looked on in dull horror.

Black splotches appeared on his face and quickly formed into letters. An 'E' shaped piece of flesh formed, and fell away, leaving a bone-deep mark behind. As it hit the floor wetly it turned into bloody foam, then immediately vanished. All of a sudden multitudes of letters started to appear all over his face and body, on his hands and in his clothes. Ten seconds later his body collapsed out of itself. Frank, only ever a figment of the imagination, was truly no more.

'It's a good thing that this house is detached, otherwise I would have the neighbours around, wondering what all the noise was,' Primrose said firmly, taking a wickedly sharp-looking paring knife from the rack on the counter. 'I'm sorry that I have to do this, but I went through several years of hell to get to where I am today, and that book is really the only thing that gives me any joy. Yes, you are... were... a *friend*; but that's my fault. I should have kept you at arm's length. But it's nice knowing an author, it feels exotic, knowing that there's someone making up whole worlds while I sit watching the television, leading a lonely old life and finding myself unable to wait for the next instalment of "The Immigrant Baby Eaters of Indo-China". Yes, it's all been rather exotic. I will do a thorough tidy of your house once you're gone and get rid of anything that might become embarrassing.' Primrose smiled briefly. Then she set about her work. She had secrets to protect.

Samantha dragged her husband's body through the house and out to the shed in the back garden. Her back screamed in agony, a pain more agonising than childbirth. But with reserves of strength she never realised she had, she managed to get him onto the work table where Frank had enjoyed tinkering with bits of wood, whittling them down into amateurish carvings of horses or owls. Already thinking ahead to the amount of bleach she would need to use to get rid of the bloody smears in the kitchen, she grabbed the saw, bought only the last year and used only the once. Its teeth were sharp and after minor resistance, started to saw off her husband's head quite adequately. The windpipe parted after one deep sweep of the saw, but the neck was trickier and needed a little more effort. But Samantha got there, and four hours later, the body was in bits and ready to be bagged up and disposed of.

Later, when Primrose was mopping the kitchen, she noticed Amie's necklace in a pool of blood on the floor. She picked it up carefully, flicking a bit of gore off it with distaste. She took it to the sink and washed the blood off; luckily it hadn't been cleaved in two with her exertions. Then an idea came to her. She dried the chain carefully and went to the ornately carved mahogany dresser, opened the drawer where the ledger had safely been returned to, and took the key for the drawer out, locked it and threaded the fine, silver chain through it. She put the necklace around her neck, her fingers forever nimble enough to work the delicate clasp. The cold black key kissed her décolletage like a conspiratorial lover. Primrose smiled and went back to cleaning the kitchen.

THE JACKET

CHARLOTTE McGARRY came in through the front door hesitantly. She put her satchel down next to the hat stand then started to tip-toe her way past the lounge to the stairs and up to the safety of the bedroom.

'Have a good day then Char?' Mother asked as she came out to see her with a smile on her face that faltered when she saw the black eye and the nasty looking cut above her daughter's eyebrow. 'What happened?' she asked, kneeling down to get a better view, stroking Charlotte's blonde hair back in comfort.

'I... I fell...' she stammered, knowing full well that she was never able to lie to Mother. She saw through everything, every time.

'Come on, you can tell me,' Mother soothed, drawing her close.

Should she tell? Would it just cause more trouble? Ever since Father had died Charlotte had always tried to take care of her own problems. She also remembered the time when Mother had complained to the schoolmaster once before, who promptly told her that boys will be boys, all rough and tumble and that Charlotte really should play with her own sex and not interfere with the games of football and bulldog. 'Skipping,' he had said patting Mother on the hand. 'Girls like skipping.'

'It was Christian Christie,' Charlotte said, matter of factly. She clenched her fists and her bottom lip started to tremble, but she kept it in, and then Mother started to cry, seeing her dead husband's resolve showing through in her little girl.

Later on they were both sitting around the battle-scarred table in the kitchen. Mother had made her a steaming mug of tea in Father's old chipped mug, and Charlotte's hands were fantastically warm as they wrapped around it.

'I wish Father was here,' Charlotte said gently. Mother nodded, a small smile appeared. Father had died in the War five years before. He had taken a bullet in France.

'Me too, dear, but in some ways he is. It's going to be the summer holidays soon; would you like to spend some time with Grandad?'

Charlotte grinned as she thought of Grandad, her Father's father. He was always full of stories and tricks and nonsense. She hadn't seen him since Christmas and it would be good to get away, and the thought of running into Christian time after time filled her with dread.

'I'd love to!' she said, taking a swig of tea and burning her tongue in the process.

The luscious green countryside dazzled Charlotte's eyes. The train was chugging its way through the Stour Valley, climbing up a slow hill, where the view would be even grander. An old book by E.F. Benson lay in her lap. The stories in it were very good, but she had quite a vivid imagination and didn't really know why Mother had packed it. The cabin was empty and had been since Effingham, and the thoughts of ghouls and ghosts seeping through the seats... well, it spooked her silly.

Three hours later and the train gently pulled into Brigham River station. Charlotte could see her Grandad waiting amongst the sparse group of people standing on the platform; over six foot tall, with a wave of brilliant white hair; there was a man who couldn't fail to be noticed wherever he went.

As soon as the train stopped, she ran to the door and hopped from one foot to the other as she waited for it to be opened. As soon as it was, she was into the arms of her laughing Grandad, who picked her up and whirled her around and around, though her feet did accidently hit the rump of a rather overweight woman who was drowning a very thin man in a striped suit with kisses. She barely noticed the disturbance.

'So how the devil are you, Mistress McGarry?' he asked once the porter had dragged off Charlotte's trunk that was around three times larger than the girl was. His thumb gently touched the yellowing under the young one's eye.

'I'm getting better all the time,' she replied. It was the truth and the old man ruffled her hair in approval.

'Good. That's all I need to know.' His face looked serious for a second as if he was going to say something, but he kept his peace. 'Let's get this old beast home, hey?' And they walked towards the car which looked as if it had taken the full force of a Doodlebug.

The drive to Three Rivers was conducted in happy silence. Charlotte was happily suffused in an affectionate glow as she recognised the various landmarks they sped past. As they pulled out past the village store, they nearly ran over a woman who was holding the hand of a young girl of around five with long ringlets. They both looked at the occupants of the car sternly, then the woman saw who it was and laughed.

'When are you going to realise that you were never one for driving, Reginald?'

'I'm sorry, Elizabeth. Won't happen again.' he said, chuckling as he drove off.

He turned to look at his granddaughter. 'That was Elizabeth Babblebrook and her daughter Anna who live up the road from me, they are both very pleasant. The husband has a lot to be said for himself though, rumour has it that he's a mean drunk, though I've never seen it.' Grandad realised what he was saying, and slapped his wide forehead with the palm of his hand. 'Have got to remember that such talk might get back to your mother!' he exclaimed.

Charlotte shook her head vehemently. 'No Grandad, you know I keep my secrets. Well, only the good ones...' Both were reminded of the time that Charlotte had let fly the fact that Grandad had let slip some gas quite noisily in church the last time the young girl had visited. Shook the font that one had. Her mother thought she would die of embarrassment if she ever had a chance to bump into the vicar.

The car wound through the lazy country lanes that escaped from the other side of town until they came to the old stone bridge that spanned the River Stone.

'I think a spot of trout fishing will definitely be in order this holiday,' Grandad said as they came to a stop on the other side of the bridge. Both got out of the battered car and Grandad went to the boot and pulled out two rods and a wicker basket. Grinning foolishly, they both jumped the dyke, making their way down the embankment until they were at the river's edge.

Dinner was very good that night.

The summer holidays flew past and Charlotte felt that there was no way that the holiday could possibly be bettered. The house, as always, was a ramshackle joy to behold; her Grandad was a serious hoarder of weird and odd nick-knacks with the latest addition to his "collection" being a shrunken head. Charlotte didn't think it was real but the nose did look incredibly sculpted and life-like. Another addition was the twisted tail fin of a German aircraft, the Nazi ensign burnt and scorched. Grandad said he had found it in the river.

Apart from all of the fishing, they hiked high into the hills until they came to Three Rivers Castle, now sadly a tumbledown of stones. But there were still things to be found, and Charlotte discovered what her Grandad wildly exclaimed was the handle of a broadsword; something that could lop off the heads of a thousand and one men.

The last night of Charlotte's holiday crept in. Both were sitting in the lounge in grand looking wingback chairs, the fire was roaring, casting leaping shadows over the walls and mounted heads of foxes, rams and deer, their glass eyes a mirror to the coldness of their deaths.

Grandad was slightly drunk, a generous helping of whisky in his hand. Charlotte was drinking homemade lemonade, the sharpness of it making her insides wince.

The older man's gaze was ever focused though. He looked at his granddaughter more seriously than he ever had before, making her uncomfortable and slightly nervous.

'So, tell me about this Christian Christie then?' It wasn't a general dilly-dally around the subject, he wanted firm answers.

So Charlotte told him. She told him how it began, when they were once actually quite friendly until the day that Charlotte had brought some marbles into school, the very same ones that her Grandad had bought her one Christmas. Jealousy or whatever monster grabbed hold of Christian, and he had demanded that Charlotte be a good friend and give them to him. When she refused, Christian had socked her on the nose, leaving the girl terribly shocked and in tears. And that was it. Overnight Christian had gone from friend to hated enemy, a name that sent cold dread up her spine every time Charlotte heard it. A face that would send her heart plummeting and scrabbling for comfort at the bottom of her stomach every time Christian was nearby. And sometimes he brought his friends along too. On more than one occasion they had all set on her, kicking her while she was down on the ground, and they were laughing and laughing...

Charlotte burst into tears. 'I just don't know what to do Grandad. Teachers won't stop him and he gets more and more angry with me. I try to fight back, I really do, but he's too big...'

Grandad stared angrily into space and swallowed the rest of his whisky in one gulp. He lurched out of his chair, dropping the crystal tumbler onto the tiger rug.

'There will be no tears in this room,' he said gently and disappeared from the lounge and into the dark hallway.

Charlotte wiped her face and laughed as she heard a curse word float into the lounge. A few minutes later and Grandad brought in an old leather suitcase that was held together by rope. He dumped it on the rug, then slowly got down next to it, his knees popping like the cracking of dry timber, and started to untie the knot.

'Come close, Char,' he said and the girl got out from the wing-back chair and knelt next to her Grandad. The old man opened the trunk.

'What do you see?' he asked his granddaughter.

'Wow! An American bomber jacket! Where did you get it from, Grandad?' Charlotte asked, reaching into the trunk and pulling it out. 'Can I...' she asked, and Grandad nodded, though a little hesitantly.

The young girl put on the jacket and it was a perfect fit, like the old man knew it would be.

'So there you have it. It's a nice jacket that, and it'll go a long way to protect you girl,' he said, getting up from his knees and reaching down to pick up the tumbler from the rug which he took to the side cabinet and poured himself another generous helping of whisky.

'What do you mean, "protect me?"'

'I mean, protect you from the cold girl, protect you from the cold. It's a thick jacket.' Grandad hurriedly took another drink, his mind spinning, wondering if he had done the right thing or not.

Later, when Charlotte had retired to bed, Reginald sat in the kitchen, where the jacket was laid out onto the table. When he had owned it, it had been a long trench jacket, and it had saved his life on more than one occasion when he was a medical officer in the trenches during the First World War.

He thought back to that day, Germans swarming all around him, bullets whizzing past his head, and then they were actually in the trenches, and he could remember the looks on their faces as they raised their rifles to shoot, the hate which quickly turned into confusion, fear, then pure, unadulterated terror...

As to where Reginald had got the jacket from, he couldn't recall; the days before the War when he volunteered were extremely blurred and misremembered. But he was wearing it on that fateful day and it had saved his life and that's all that mattered. But the fact that it had turned into a bomber jacket for the girl? Reginald got up, he was going to tell Charlotte that the coat wasn't for her, wasn't for girls and that Christian would in all probability try and steal it off her, which would be very bad indeed.

Fool of an old man! What were you thinking..?

He cried out sharply as his foot caught the corner of the trunk and he fell forwards, the stone hearth of the kitchen fireplace rushing up to meet him.

The journey back to Effingham on the Stour was one of the most desolate journeys Charlotte had ever had to make in her life. Mother sat next to her, her face all puffy and swollen; the tears they had both shed could have filled the Municipal Pool.

To think that Grandad had been lying there all night. It tore Charlotte's heart in two that she hadn't heard anything. She had found him, and there had been a lot of blood; Charlotte didn't realise a blow to the head could produce that much blood. She had started to cry, sob and scream and it wasn't until the local Bobby had heard her when he was doing his morning rounds that she stopped. She stayed with Elizabeth Babblebrook until Mother came to organise things.

She was wrapped up in the bomber jacket, and that was good— the smell of it didn't really remind her of him though—he had never smelt of bubblegum for one thing. But the fact that he had given it to her, and had been the last act of kindness he had shown... she would never take it off, she promised herself, and hadn't, not even at the funeral.

Home felt strange, alien and all the tea in the world that Mother made couldn't comfort her. She felt as listless and as grey as the weather which had turned for the worst after weeks upon weeks of beautiful sunshine.

There were three more days to go before the start of school, and Charlotte didn't want to go, *begged* Mother not to make her go. Mother had hesitated and actually went to the headmaster's house to talk to Professor Monty James about taking Charlotte out for a couple of weeks until she came to her senses a little more. But James wouldn't have any of it and threatened everything bar the fire and brimstone if Charlotte wasn't there for the first day's lessons.

In the end Charlotte only said that she would go if she could wear the bomber jacket. Mother wearily agreed, but only if she actually took the jacket off while in class. So, on that Monday morning, Charlotte left home and walked through the field towards the river where she would walk towards town for the half a mile it would take her to get to Effingham Elementary School. Her mind was far away, fishing with her Grandad, replaying some of their best catches together. She didn't know if she would ever, *could* ever fish again. Maybe one day, when she felt...

'Hello there, Charlotte. Nice jacket. I want it,' Christian said, coming up from behind, grabbing her arm and squeezing really hard. 'It's the kind of jacket I would look good in, and certainly something that shouldn't be given to a girl to wear.' There was low menace in his voice and Charlotte's body was drenched in cold fear, she knew that if she had to fight for the jacket, it would be done as dirty as she was able.

Then her vision went bright, stars danced in front of her eyes, then went monochrome, then static. She fell to her knees. Christian kicked her in the stomach, she cried out and fell onto her back. Then another kick, this time to her face, she thought her cheek might be broken.

Her vision swam back into a semblance of focus, Christian, dank brown hair and lazy eye, his face an almost comedic mask of violence. He reached into his pocket and pulled out a small knife. Charlotte coughed, and a spatter of blood landed on the jacket, and seemed to soak straight through the thick fabric and disappeared.

'Now, you bitch,' said Christian. 'I want that jacket, and even if I have to cut it from you, I will.'

Charlotte kicked out, taking Christian off-guard and she forced herself up from the dirt and stood her ground as Christian regained his composure, his face now betraying the signs of pure hatred. He thrust his knife hand forward and the blade vanished into the folds of the jacket. Charlotte felt no pain, only a thudding contact. They both heard a chomping, snapping sound. The young boy screamed as he pulled back his hand; correction, what was *left* of his hand. He stared incomprehensibly at the bloodied stump that was jettisoning his life fluid everywhere.

Charlotte looked down at the jacket in near madness, only the thought of her Grandad giving it to her to protect her kept the young girl from tipping over the edge.

Christian took a few steps back, then fell onto his behind. Charlotte felt suddenly sorry for him. She kneeled down to him and hugged him, unmindful of his screams and she hugged him tighter and the jacket started to chomp deeply into his flesh, destroying his face, tearing out his windpipe; devouring him slowly until not even the sun that shone out of his behind was left.

After Christian was gone Charlotte realised that the jacket felt heavy, felt sated—and even though she was scared by what she had done, she knew she would be fine, she would never be caught and she thanked her Grandad for loving her enough to want to help sort out her problems.

In time she changed, and so too, did the jacket.

'I WISH'

'MA DEID DUGS.'

'Wha'?' Andy Wharton raised his eyebrow at the drunk at the bar, who was swaying back and forth. Andy was surprised that he hadn't fallen over. *Must hae a steedy compass then,* he mused, waiting for the drunk to speak again.

'I luv ma deid dugs. Ah hiv thir skulls oan the mantelpiece.' The drunk began to cry and *then* promptly fell over, hitting his head on the floor. He moaned once and was still.

'Barmaid, yer goan tae hiv tae see tae yer man here,' Andy shouted through to the girl who was out back, smoking a tab, before draining off the last of his pint of Stella. He nudged the drunk with his foot.

'Ye micht hiv tae ring fir an ambulance.'

He put on his thick jacket and walked out into the rain.

He had been back in the country for twenty-four hours and although he had left Afghanistan and the horrors behind, he would rather be there than here.

Possilpark. *Forever* a shitehole.

Andy walked away from the pub, up the hill that took him past the bookies and the Spar shop.

'Oi!'

Andy kept walking.

'Oi! You, ya bam, git yer fucking airse ower *here* NOW!'

Andy stopped, his hand going for the handle of the knife that was tucked down the back waistband of his jeans.

He turned around and saw the drunk weaving his way towards him, blood running down his face.

'It wiz YOU who killt ma dugs!'

The red mist descended and Andy took two steps forward, grabbed the drunk by his dirty shirt collar and nutted him, relishing the crunch as his forehead broke an already battered looking nose.

'*OhfuckinghellyabassartmafuckingBEAK!*' the drunkard squealed, running quite ably in the direction of the pub. Andy didn't think he would receive much sympathy there.

As Andy walked away he looked up at the tower blocks but couldn't see the tops of them for the filthy mist that always seemed to hang around, even on the days it didn't rain.

The entrance to the tower block looked like the one of the openings to hell itself. As soon as he pushed the door open, the smell of piss and shit hit him, but he didn't gag; he had smelt far, far worse in Afghanistan.

Two youths sat on the third level, passing a party-sized bottle of White Lightning between them. A pouch of Amber Leaf, a packet of skins and a half-ounce of grass lay at their feet. They watched Andy warily, but said nothing as he climbed the stairs.

Andy's brother lived right at the top, free from most of the problems of the tower block, mostly because whoever was causing the trouble couldn't be arsed to climb up that far. The lift had been put out of commission the first week people had started moving in.

The green door had a notice taped to it. *NO JUNK MAIL.* Someone had tampered with it so it read 'No Junky Males'.

He knocked on the door twice, then bent down and shouted through the letterbox.

'Morris, its yer brother. Let us in.'

The flat was warm and immaculately kept. Sheila, Morris' wife was in the kitchen, dishing up lasagne. The two brothers drank whisky from mugs and watched Luke, Morris' seven year old, play Modern Warfare 3 on the PS3.

'Yir no sayin' much,' Morris noted, finishing off his mug and pouring himself another generous helping.

'No much tae say.'

'Ye look rough.'

'Cheers.' Andy said.

'Nae worries.' Morris smiled.

Sheila came through with a dinner tray for Andy. He nodded his thanks and started to eat.

'Luke, turn that machine oaf and git yir dinner,' Morris told him. Luke huffed, but did as he was told.

They ate in silence. After dinner, smoking a cigarette, Andy looked out of the window. The street lights far below were just noticeable through the gloom.

'Ye'll be wanting the couch the night then?' Sheila asked him as they all sat round the telly, watching *Eastenders*.

'If ye dinnae mind, only fir the night. Ah'll be awa' in the morning. Ah'll stay wi' a pal in Edinburgh till I hiv tae git back.'

'You goin' back tae kill the ragheids?' Luke asked.

'Luke!' Sheila scudded the boy across the head. He yelped indignantly.

'Maw, that's no fair! A'body calls them that at school!'

'And I brocht ye up wi' better manners than that. Ye want tae go tae bed early?' she threatened.

'No maw.' Luke jumped on the sofa between his dad and his uncle, the chiding already forgotten. 'Uncle Andy, did ye hiv to shoot anyone, like in MW3?'

Now it was Morris' turn. 'Right laddie, off tae bed with ye. Leave yir Uncle alone.'

'There wir wan or two wee tight spoats ah hid tae git masell oot o,' Andy allowed the boy before he was dragged off to his room.

'You'll hiv seen it oan the news then,' Andy asked, looking at the pair of them. He had moved down to the gas fire, where Luke normally sat, killing his pixelated terrorists.

'Aye. Yir lucky maw still isnae wi us. She'd have hud the cat *and* the kittens by noo,' Morris smiled, pulling a B&H from its packet and lighting it up.

'Ah should be deid, yet ah walked away wi nary a scratch.'

'Whit happened?' Sheila asked quietly.

'We wir east o' Kandahar, ten o' us, eight yanks and twenty Afghani sodjiers. Deid o' night and aw o' a sudden it's fuckin' *chaos*. Sky lights up like it's fuckin' Christmas an' whoever wiz firin' at us, fuck it wiz coming at us frae aw directions. We tail it tae this irrigation trench. Wi dinnae ken how mony o' the bastards there wir and some o' the Afghani cunts that wir taggin along wi us fucked aff and left us in deep shit. An' we said we'd keep oan fighting till every yin o' us wiz deid. Well, they wirnae wrang there. I wiz the last yin staundin'. Ah managed tae creep through the numpties firing at us and git tae safety.'

'How the fuck did ye manage tae walk away frae that?' Morris asked, incredulously.

'I sacrificed a'body.' Andy said simply. He reached across for the bottle of whisky and poured a full mug and started drinking deeply.

'Ye whit?'

'I did a deal wi' the wee man. Ah sacrificed ma pals an a'body else as weel.'

'Sacrificed ma airse,' Morris said angrily. 'Whit kind o' talk is that? Ye got lucky. That's aw.'

Andy got up and walked to the dining table where his jacket was hung up on the back of one of the chairs. He pulled out a battered Golden Virginia tobacco tin, opened the lid and offered it to his brother who wrinkled his nose with distaste.

'Whit the fuck is *that*?' the older brother asked. 'A hen's fit?'

'Naw, that's a monkey's paw. I bought it frae some roadside beggar the first week I was oot there. I did it fir a laugh really. He said that it wid gie the bearer o' the paw three wishes. He wiz deadly serious though.' Andy's voice dropped to a whisper. 'He said ah could only buy it if ah truly believed in magic.'

'And ye said *aye*? Are ye a fucking daftie?'Sheila said, taking the paw from Morris and staring at it intently.

'In the back o' ma mind there wiz always the thocht that if ah ever goat deep in the shite, it might just git me oot o' it.' Andy said. 'Call it mumbo jumbo, I ken that aw ma mates did... but they're aw deid, and ahm still staunding.'

'So gettin' oot o' that gunfight, wiz that yir first wish, or last yin?' Sheila twirled the paw round betwixt thumb and forefinger, raising it up to her nose for a sniff.

'Ma first. When the bullets first stairted flyin', I got oot the paw, clasped it tightly and wished that no hairm came to me. I walked awa' frae that turkey shoot wi no even a scratch. Ah believe in it a lot mair noo, than afore, I kin tell ye.'

He reached across and plucked the paw from Sheila's hand. She suddenly seemed loathe to give it up. Andy put it back in his tin and closed it up.

The next morning after Andy left, Sheila was heading down the stairs so she could go to the post office to get the child benefits when saw the paw lying on the floor of the fifth level. She stopped, knowing what it was immediately, her heart slamming in her chest.

She approached it cautiously, half expecting it to scuttle away as she went to pick it up. She shook her head at her own timidity.

It's deid. Where's it goan tae go?

She was pretty sure that Andy had put the top back on the baccy tin pretty firmly. *Maybe no' as firm as he thocht.* She picked it up, opening up her purse and popped it in. She was sure that Andy'd be back for it – he wasn't going to leave his good luck charm behind.

That evening, she tried to phone Andy's mobile without any luck—it just rang straight to answerphone. She took the paw out and put it on the dining table.

Morris eyed it suspiciously. 'Di ye think that the bullshit Andy said really happened? Ye nivver ken with these foreigners and their hoodoo voodoo,' he said, prodding the paw with his finger.

'So that's where Luke's gettin' his racist crap frae then? I wullnae fuckin' tolerate it Morris, it's no oan.'

'Come oan hen, ahm sorry, I wiz jist kidding.'

Sheila grabbed for the paw, held it tight in her hand, closed her eyes and said out loud, 'Ah wish for a life-changing amount o' money so we can git the fuck oot o' here,' and as soon as the words were out, she screamed and threw the mummified paw on the table.

'Whit the fuck did ye dae that fir?' Morris asked. 'Ye want tae wake up the lad?'

'It *moved*! It twisted in ma hand as soon as ah said ah wanted the money!' Sheila's face was chalk white.

'Dinnae be daft, yer only imagining it. Heat's turned ye funny. And life-changing amount o' money? You been watching too much *This Morning*.' Morris laughed bitterly, picked up the monkey's paw and went into the kitchen and put it in the bin.

'I suppose,' Sheila whispered.

She hit the gin pretty heavily that night.

'Kin we go tae McDonalds the morns morn maw?' Luke asked, munching into Coco-Pops like there was no tomorrow.

'Only if ye promise tae dae yer haimwork and ye dinnae play yir faither up like ye hiv been daen this week,' Sheila warned, grabbing his lunchbox and putting it into his schoolbag. Her hangover was merciless; punishing her for the previous evening's session.

'Ah promise Maw.'

Morris came through from the bedroom, kissed Sheila on the cheek and slapped her arse.

'Good lad,' she ruffled his hair and grinned until a thump of pain hit her right between the eyes.

A buffet of wind rocked the building making the room tremble ever so slightly.

'Yet anither lovely day in sunny Possilpark!' Morris chirped, getting Luke's jacket and helping the lad into it.

Luke grinned and pointed out at the black sky and shook his head, *uh-huh* and laughed.

'Ye want me tae walk ye tae school the day son?'

'Nah, it's a'right Da', Billy and his Maw are gonna meet me doonstairs and we'll walk tae school thegither.'

'Be safe,' Sheila called out to him as he left the flat.

Fifteen minutes later he was dead.

Luke's too small coffin sat on a plinth at the head of the church. Sheila was on as much temazepam as she could get inside her. She hadn't uttered a word since Billy's mother said (in true schemie fashion) something to her that made her feel sick ever time she thought about it.

'The compo' the cooncil ur goantae hiv tae pay oot tae ye wull be astronomical. At least that'll be somethin'...'

Andy didn't turn up, even though he had said he would. He'd sounded like a broken man when Morris had told him the news. He kept on promising that he would be there for the pair of them as soon as he could get out of going back to Afghanistan. He didn't ask about the monkey's paw. He didn't need to.

As the coffin was taken to the cemetery, the sun broke free of the clouds, and shone, for a while.

After the wake, Morris and Sheila sat in the kitchen, drinking straight vodkas. Eastenders droned softly in the background. A letter from the council was on the table in front of them, saying that an enquiry would be held and any compensation would be awarded sooner, rather than later.

'I want him back so fuckin' badly,' Sheila cried. Her eyes were glazed, her face slack with the toils of the last week.

Morris had his head in his hands. After a while he looked up at her. 'If it wisnae fir that fuckin' wish, Luke wid still be wi' us noo.'

She screamed. 'It wiz your fuckin' brother an' fuckin' his tales o' black magic! How wis I supposed to ken? Ah jist wanted awthing tae be guid fur wance...'

Sheila got up abruptly and ran through to the bedroom coming back with the monkey's paw in her hand.

'Ah thocht ah threw that oot?' Morris yelled. 'Gie it tae me *right* now Sheila. Yiv caused enough trouble a'ready.'

Sheila had a faraway look in her eyes. 'We can bring him back, we can bring oor boy back.'

Before Morris could reach her she closed her eyes and wished.

The paw twisted in her hands as she mouthed words that Morris couldn't quite hear. She opened her eyes and cried out triumphantly.

He made a grab for the hand that was holding the paw. 'Try it, jist goan an' try it,' she hissed 'Ah'll scratch yir eyes oot o' yir skull.'

Morris sat back down on the chair. He talked slowly and clearly so she would understand every word. 'He's been deid ten days now hen. They tellt us how much o' a mess he wis in when that wa' fell on him. Dae ye really want him back like that?'

'Ah'll always love him, no matter whit.'

They waited. The hands slowly crawled around the clock face. After a while, Sheila slumped in her chair. Morris helped her to her bed but she wouldn't give up the paw.

Outside, the wind howled and the rain spattered against the window. Morris lay in bed, smoking.

He heard a low scrape echo in the stairwell, a noise that would be inaudible to anyone other than those who lived in the tower. But of course, no-one would go to see what it was.

There was a louder scrape, followed by a heavy thump. Climbing up the stairs, higher and higher, level after level.

And soon, whatever it was...

...would be at the door.

Morris got up and padded silently to the door and looked out of the spyglass. There was nobody there. He slid down the door and knelt there, his ear against the wood. He thought he could hear breathing, low, ragged, shallow.

A knock, a loud one, filled the stairwell.

Sheila burst out the bedroom, taking Morris by surprise and knocking him flat on his back. 'Luke? It's yer maw. Come to yer maw, son.'

In her haste to open up the three deadbolts and turn the key, she dropped the paw she had been clutching all night.

Morris leapt for it. He grabbed hold of the paw, closed his eyes and wished, just as Sheila turned the door handle.

The paw flashed white heat, danced in his fist, felt like a fish trying to escape the clutches of its captor. He dropped it. Sheila wailed with agony as the door swung open. There was nobody there. The smell of fresh dirt and embalming fluid filled the air. Sheila fled down the stairs and into the storm outside, her dressing gown flapping around her as she shouted into the wind again and again.

'Luke? It's yer Maw. Come tae yer Maw.'

Morris looked down at the entrance to his home. A child's leather shoe, the kind you'd wear if you went to posh school, sat on the welcome mat.

> "They hardly exchanged a word, for now
> they had nothing to talk about."
>
> *The Monkey's Paw* – W.W. Jacobs

GEORGE V

'G UID AIFTERNOON SIR and welcome tae the Lichthoose,' the antiques dealer said in his soft Highland brogue as a dishevelled Elias walked into the shop.

'Good afternoon,' Elias replied, looking around as if he didn't know what he was after. 'Postcards, I collect old postcards. Do you have any?'

'Through the back here. Follae me. I hae about ten fodders fu' o' them. Aroond whit period di ye prefer?'

'Around the nineteen-hundreds mark?'

The dealer led Elias through a dark passageway to a back room which held all sorts of junk and furniture—a stuffed bear, ceramics and on top of a small bookcase at the back, five folders and three biscuit tins full of postcards. Elias smiled at the dealer who went back through to his desk to finish the crossword and a lukewarm cup of tea.

After he had left, Elias took out his small magnifying glass and started looking through the postcards. Half an hour later he took a large bundle through to the elderly chap, who squinted at them thoughtfully.

'So, why postcards frae this time then, son?'

'I like to frame them—there's something about that time which was just so simple,' Elias lied, his heart thudding quickly in his chest.

The dealer had asked for forty pounds for the two hundred postcards, Elias handed over the crumpled notes then left with his trove and walked down the wide market street to the cafe at the end of the road next to Barclays. He ordered a cup of tea and a slice of carrot cake and after they had arrived, took out the postcards and a magnifying glass to start studying the stamps that were on the back of them.

He started to weep.

Elias and his father fell out over stamps. Jacob had fallen on hard times ever since he had retired and try as he might, could not find the George V halfpenny stamp. It was the only stamp in the whole world both men had an interested in, and they scoured all of the charity shops, antiques dealers and car boot fairs they went to in their quest for them. Elias on the other hand was having a run of luck, finding two 'Downey Heads', the stamp's nickname, at a postcard fair in Colchester. Jacob visited Elias' one night, brought round a bottle of whisky and the two men talked of old times. They talked about Sheila, Elias' mother, then on to how they started to look for the stamps after Jacob met a collector in a pub. The man had told him the history of the George V halfpenny stamp, that there may have been two hundred sheets of rogue stamps printed with a missing perforation instead of the normal fifteen perforations that usually lined each. This particular one had fourteen and it wasn't noticed until quite late—the sheets were recalled and destroyed. The fifteen "perf" stamp itself was only issued for eighteen months. With that, the search had begun.

The two men continued drinking until the early hours and finally Elias gave in and went to bed. When he woke up the next morning; his father had gone and so had the two postcards with the stamps on them from his top drawer in the bedroom. When he confronted him, his dad refused to apologise, saying that had he asked Elias for a loan and would have probably turned him down. An outraged Elias said that wasn't the point and the argument hit nuclear proportions.

Three years passed without the two men passing a civil word to each other and then suddenly, Jacob died. Elias thought he was strong enough not to feel the pain, that the betrayal would carry enough bile in his belly for him to coast through for the next twenty years or so. But the pain was there, he had loved his father so much but the stupid stubbornness in him meant that he couldn't let it go—to him this love made the betrayal feel all the more keen.

He continued to hunt all over the country for the stamps; the hunt was made all the more interesting for Elias by the fact that many of the sheets were sent to the East Anglian coast and were posted from the Great Yarmouth area. Holidaymakers sent postcards to relatives and friends all over the United Kingdom. Elias didn't know how many there were or where they would turn up.

He had spent the last five years on the road, ever since his father had died; going from town to town to the many antiques shops and centres to ask if they had any old postcards. Postcards were collectible in themselves and if a shop owner saw that Elias spent more time looking at the back than the front of the card and asked why, Elias had a several stories ready—one being that he was a historian and loved looking for odd sounding names. These explanations would generally appease and Elias was always thankful that dealers didn't know everything and that the stamps would, in the main, go unnoticed until he stumbled across them. He would pay pennies for the postcards, leave the shop putting them in his plastic folder, then travel to the next town.

Elias lived a frugal life while on the road—he hitchhiked and walked everywhere, slept in his tent, didn't drink or smoke and would only go back to Norwich after he had found ten to twenty postcards with the stamps on. His house, on the outskirts of town, was his own, so it was easy to mothball the place until it was time to return. He would take his stamps to the local dealer who would, if the fourteen perforations were present and correct and the postmark on the stamp was a clean one, give up to four-hundred pounds per stamp.

He spent his winters reading and waiting for spring to come back round so he could go out searching once more.

Elias was in a bookshop in Cromer, spending the day milling around and waiting for spring to fully show her hand again so he could go start over. His feet were itching and he wanted to be back on the open road, but the winter was a severe one and showed no sign of letting up. The money he had saved from the stamps was starting to dwindle, though things weren't getting desperate *yet*. Elias was in the Second World War section and pulled out a paperback that he had been searching for, for quite a while called *The Lion Has Wings* by John Ware. He opened the book and a postcard spilled out onto the floor. He bent down to pick up the familiar shape and as always, looked at the back before the front.

There was a Downey Head on it. He quickly counted the perforations, his heart thudding in his chest. Fourteen of them! Elias laughed, stunned at this million to one find. But he would take fortune where he found it, four hundred quid was not to be sniffed at. He quickly scanned the writing on the card.

> *Dear E,*
> *Let me apologise and let me make right my*
> *wrong. Visit the Lighthouse in Tongue, that's*
> *where I will seek my forgiveness.*
> *Love always,*
> *Your father,*
> *Jacob.*

His mind reeling, Elias scanned the post date. Things were getting stranger. It was sent on the exact day his father had died, but a hundred years previously. Even the handwriting was spookily familiar, though his father had always looped his J's. Elias tucked the postcard back into the book and took it to the front of the shop. On the way home in the bus he stared at his find, unable to take his eyes away from it. He didn't know why, but it was pushing at his buttons, and surely this was a coincidence too far.

An internet search did indeed reveal an antiques shop called

The Lighthouse in Tongue. It was over six hundred and eighty five miles away; a marathon hitchhike, something that he had never attempted before. And in this weather, it would probably end up killing him. Elias went to the cemetery where his father lay and sat there in silence for a good hour, it was the first time he had been to his grave. As he got up, he placed the postcard next to the simple wooden cross; there hadn't been any money to pay for a proper headstone.

'Okay dad, I'll go.'

The next day Elias locked his front door, stuck the keys in his pocket and trudged down the snowy drive until he got the roadside. He hefted up his rucksack, laden with tent, four seasons sleeping bag and cooking equipment and stuck out his thumb as the first car passed.

'Guid aifternoon sir and welcome tae the Lichthoose,' the antiques dealer said in his soft Highland brogue as a very dishevelled Elias walked into the shop.

Elias smiled.

THE WERE-DWARF

VINNY DAZZLE CAME OUT of the Florden Arms lugging a
metal case that was almost as big as he was. The night, as far
as the drinking populace was concerned, had been an unquantifi-
able success when he'd stuck on *Dancing Queen* and *The Time Warp*
back to back for the encore. Vinny was into hard house himself,
but money was money, and as Norfolk's premier DJ, his tune
spinning and witty banter was in demand from every landlord of a
hostelry on the great plain of East Anglia.

Vinny had first come to the public's eye two years previously,
when he'd featured on Channel Four's *Wife Swap*. He was paired
with the wife of Britain's tallest man. At just a hair over three foot
himself, Vinny was the UK's smallest adult male. This particular
episode garnered much controversy due to footage showing Vinny
taking over Cameron "Slam Dunk" Davies' daytime job as player/
coach of the Norwich Knights basketball team. The scene in
question captured one of the players picking up Vinny (as he was
holding the ball) only to throw him and it through the hoop. It
caused outrage amongst human rights activists, but it gave Vinny
cult status; the clip being viewed on Youtube over five hundred
thousand times in a week.

In the months that followed he was thrust into the very eye of
the media storm. He gave interviews to newspapers and appeared
on *This Morning* and *The Paul O' Grady* show—where he proved
himself to be a highly intelligent and witty chap. The public took
to him all the more when three months into his fame, his wife
Mary, a woman of average size, died whilst being chased by a
reporter as she left her local butchers. She had bought a couple of
t-bone steaks for dinner and was cornered. She tried to escape—

running out into the road without looking, only to be hit by the Number 30 Darsham bus. Photos of Vinny crying next to his wife's hospital bed, his gentle hand cradling hers, burned affection into the hearts and minds of a nation. Activist groups for people of small stature hailed him a role model (never knowing about the coke habit he'd had since leaving school at seventeen).

Apart from this insatiable habit, one that none of his new found friends knew about, Vinny appeared a different kind of celebrity. He shunned the quick buck and front page coverage; refusing to turn up to red carpet events and the inevitable invites to openings. He only agreed to the shoot for *OK* magazine to raise money for the local children's hospice. It was down the road from where he lived.

But none of this was helping Vinny with his everyday frustrations as he dragged the heavy box full of treasured 45s across the car park to his East German Trabant—a good distance away from the pub. The Florden was known for harbouring the kind of clientele that would piss on cars with gay abandon when the gents became too hard to find or its floor too wet to remain upright. It had been a particularly trying night as he'd had to ward off the affections of the landlord's overfriendly Bull Mastiff, Vindaloo—a dog that seemed to think Vinny was fair game. Finally, on reaching the car, he unlocked the boot and hefted his metal case in with a grunt, swept back a stray hair from his face and returned to the pub to get the decks. Vindaloo was waiting for him, panting heavily.

'Fucked if I'm ever going back to that pub again,' Vinny swore as he drove deep into the Norfolk countryside, sticking on *Hardcore Massive Volume 19* and cranking up the volume until his eardrums started to thrum. His newly pressed trousers were pressed no longer and there was a suspicious stain on one leg that would take some cleaning. Being as small as he was had its problems. Drunks lifted him up and stuck him on coat hooks and jokers placed their pints on his head. But since he'd become a celebrity of sorts, he was getting much more respect... and the money was getting better. Still, he wasn't going back to that pu...

His Trabant sputtered, lurched and he managed to pull it over onto the side of the road before it died.

'Fuckshitcuntwankbollocks!' he screamed, slamming the steering wheel with both hands. He looked at the place where there had never been a petrol gauge. He'd forgotten about counting the miles per gallon. His headlights barely lit up the road ahead. There was no petrol station behind him where the pub was, and he couldn't remember if there was one further down the road towards the A140 and home. He opened the door and slid off the boosted seat that enabled him to see over the dashboard. He pulled a packet of crumpled cigarettes from his top pocket, retrieved one and lit it, grimacing as the harsh smoke burned his lungs. He reached into the car, pulled out the keys and locked the door— which was a misnomer, as anyone with half a brain cell could still get into it.

He breathed in deeply and decided to walk back to the pub. The landlord, Kevin, was a good guy and would let him sleep on the couch until morning. He would even put up with a randy Vindaloo. He started to walk down the road, glad that the moon had come out from behind the clouds and lit up the road in front of him. By his calculations the pub was about three miles away, a breeze for someone who was bigger than he was. But he'd reach it no problem.

Half a mile in he started to become a little paranoid. The road had a line of trees on either side of it, and he could only see the first row, silver birch, bark glowing in the pale light of the full moon. Far off in the distance an owl hooted, a mournful sound that filled Vinny with the tingling of real fear.

'Don't be stupid,' he said, just wanting to hear his voice sounding calm and reassuring. It did not. Then from the woods to his left, came a loud crack, like someone standing on a branch. Vinny stood still, frantically reaching for the Swiss army knife in his pocket. He opened up the blade, which he had sharpened down to a nice edge, as he used it to make chess figures. It was a hobby he had taken up in his teens, and he had made hundreds of figurines. Bishops were his favourite to do—he absolutely hated making rooks.

Another crack. This time closer.

'I'll cut you up,' he cried shrilly, not believing a word he said.

Then suddenly, a low growl, and Vinny was slammed off the road and into the woods on the other side. He screamed as he felt something very sharp tear into his right arm, and with his left he blindly slashed out with his penknife. It made contact with soft flesh. It was probably that which saved him from getting his throat torn out. The thing that had him, let out a hellish yowl and fled into the woods, branches snapping and tearing off as it retreated further and further into the forest.

Vinny lay there, his heart galloping wildly, threatening to burst out of his chest and after a while he got up, crying with pain when he tried to move his arm. It was heavy and he could feel blood dribble from whatever wound he'd received. As he staggered onto the road, he heard it drip onto the hard surface. Sharp flashes of pain ran up his leg, and he felt an urgent sickness spread through his stomach.

What the fuck had that been? His brain was flooded with incoherent half-images as he dragged his way back to the car. He thought he had seen a snarling muzzle, long and gaunt, behind it deep black eyes.

It was like nothing on earth he had ever seen before.

He saw the shadow of his car in the distance briefly as his vision lurched drunkenly to the left and he fell onto his face, safely ensconced in the dark of his unconsciousness.

'Welcome back,' a female voice spoke softly.

Vinny opened up his eyes, his vision badly blurred.

'Where am I?' he croaked.

'You're in hospital. You've had a bit of an accident, I'm afraid.' The voice drifted across to him, and tailed off as Vinny slid into the sanctuary of darkness once more.

'Can you remember anything about what happened?'

Vinny was sitting upright now, his arm in a cast. The female who had spoken to him on his first venture back to reality turned out to be Annie Wilkies, a nurse who had been working at the hospital for around five years. She recognised Vinny immediately when he was first brought in. She'd thought him a lovely man whenever he was on the telly. She was there every time Vinny came to, and from her he managed to discover most of what happened.

What Annie hadn't been told was that the local vicar, driving back from one of his parishioner's homes after the death of the grandmother in the household, had seen something in the middle of the road and braked just in time to prevent one of God's creatures meeting its maker earlier than intended. Getting out he saw Vinny, who he had at first thought was a child. He had continued to think that way until a packet of cigarettes fell from Vinny's pocket onto the road. Three minutes later the ambulance arrived, carrying the deceased octogenarian—she was taken out and shoved in the back seat of the Vicar's car so Vinny could receive the medical attention he needed. In the light of the back of the ambulance, his wounds were clear to both the shocked driver and attendant. A deep slash was running from his shoulder, curving down his arm to end at the knuckle of his pinkie finger.

The surgeon who'd been drafted in to repair the tear had done a fine job, and Vinny counted himself lucky he hadn't lost his arm every time Annie removed his dressings to clean and re-dress his wound. It was an ugly mess and he hoped his disc spinning career wouldn't be harmed.

'So what do you think happened to you?' Annie asked, concern lighting up her face. She was really quite pretty.

Vinny shook his head. He couldn't remember anything.

'Whatever it was certainly didn't like the taste of me!' he chuckled, trying to shift in his bed, and crying out as he banged his arm. Annie came across and steadied him. Their eyes met and Annie smiled.

'You'll be fine, I'll be here whenever you want me, okay?' Annie brushed his hand, and an electric thrill travelled up his good arm.

On the day he left hospital, Vinny put on his jeans, which were still dappled with dried blood. He was given a new top by Annie at his behest. His arm was in a sling, and after much tussle and cursing, he managed to get his trousers on. He reached into his pocket and paused. He brought out his penknife, and stared at the thick black fur that was caught between the blade and the handle of the knife. He stared at it; fear prickling up his neck once more and wondered what the hell it was he was attacked by. A wild boar? Afterwards he threw the knife into a bin and tried vainly to forget.

At home, weeks after he was discharged, Vinny was doing well at taking it easy. The press had got wind that he had been in an accident but one quick call to his agents and they had come up with a suitable story. He had broken down in the middle of nowhere, he had waited in the pitch dark for a couple of hours, a car came by, he had tried to flag it down, but the car hit him and he was flung into the road. It was no-one's fault as he'd been foolish enough to stand there and his only wish was to let the driver know he was ok. The bruises on his face were such that the public swallowed it hook line and sinker. The last thing he needed was a news report supposing he'd been attacked by a fox or some other nocturnal creature. It was bad enough being small in the first place without opening himself up for ridicule. Vinny briefly scouted the online forums of *The Sun* and *The Mirror* to gauge the public's reaction—most were sending him good wishes. There were a couple of trolls writing that "allowing a minor to cross a dangerous road after bedtime was bound to result in an accident."

Later in the evening, whilst writing an email to Chico of *Chico Time* fame about a charity concert for the Ipswich children's hospice, a !Ping! alerted him to a new email. Saving his email as a draft, he was delighted to see that Annie had sent him a message. He had given her his email on a whim, knowing that his size made most women run to the hills. He had thought that Annie might be different. He was right:

> *Dear Vinny,*
>
> *I hope that your arm is getting better and that you're changing, or getting someone to change the dressing regularly. The last thing that you need is for an infection to get into it! I know that I might have appeared quiet when you asked me if I'd like to go for a drink sometime—I was just taken aback, nobody has really asked me on a date before, but I'd like to accept. Why not give me a phone to arrange a time? Number is 07916 158732.*
>
> *Hope to hear from you later then,*
> *Annie*
> *xx*

Vinny let out a whoop of joy and walked through to the kitchen to grab a beer from the fridge. Opening it, he paused, looking at the hand that was holding the can. His fingers seemed longer than they were last week. Being a man of smaller stature, small fingers were the curse of all curses, they made simple everyday tasks quite challenging. Vinny grinned—as good a time as any to be having a growth spurt he thought wryly.

The town was dead; everyone was watching the England vs. Germany match on the telly. Vinny loved his football, but when Annie had announced that she wasn't particularly keen on the beautiful game, Vinny had weighed up his options. Dinner and drinks with a beautiful woman (who may or may not want to go to bed with him) or stay at home, watching the Germans kick ten different colours of shit out of an aging squad, managed by someone who looked like he'd fallen out of the arse of a crocodile. No contest.

For his attire, Vinny had called and asked for the services of Morning Britain's fashion host Gurpreet Gondol, or Gondola to his mates. Gondola had come around instantly, joking about going to Baby Gap and wonderful rompers for him to jolly around in, but as soon as he saw the serious look in his friend's eyes, Gondola gasped then smiled. Vinny had fallen in love.

'Who is it then, Vin?' the handsome Indian asked, opening a suit carrier he had brought with him. Inside were several pieces he had "borrowed" from the storehouses at the studios, only to doctor and shorten beyond repair. Vin was pacing around, for some reason his house felt strange to him, the space that he used to feel overwhelmed in was beginning to feel like... a prison cell.

'She's a nurse, called Annie, and she sorted me out when I... I was hit,' Vinny said carefully. 'What's really *refreshing* about her is that she doesn't seem to see me as a small person.' Vinny had never or would ever call himself a midget, dwarf, wee fella or any other kind of term that was used for people of his slight stature. 'She really digs me, gets me for who I am, and that's something I've not had from a female, well ever since my wife died I suppose.'

Gondola smiled a warm smile, and placed his hand on his friends shoulder and gave it a squeeze. 'I really, really hope that it works out for you, my mini-muffin,' he laughed, then turned away and pulled a beautiful looking suit off from the rack. 'Six hundred pounds this one cost, and if you don't get laid, I'll eat my beard!'

Vinny looked at his watch. Annie was ten minutes late. With a heavy heart he turned to go, but out of the corner of his eye, he saw the nurse running precariously towards him in high heels. Now if anything was going to make him feel like a 'midget' *that* was, he grinned ruefully to himself.

'I'm so sorry I'm late,' she gasped, trying to get her breath back. 'My car broke down about half a mile away and I was trying to phone your mobile but I think it's been switched off?'

'Oh bollocks, has it?' Vinny nervously fumbled the phone out of his pocket and gave it a few taps. 'Bloody Nokias. Anyway,' he looked up at Annie who was wearing a very simple white dress with a red rose splashed over the left breast.

'You look really pretty this evening, Annie,' Vinny said, making the nurse blush. She pretended to shoo him away and then they both walked off down the road to the Italian restaurant run by one of Vinny's good friends, Marcos. He gave them the best table in the place and a fine bottle of wine, 'to make the angels sing!' he declared in a melodic accent.

They had a good evening; Vinny was in ebullient form, but he tried to slow down his frenetic pace as much as possible. He'd even foregone the Charlie. Annie was quiet but attentive—laughing when she needed to laugh and genuinely not caring about Vinny's diminutive stature. After the meal, they went for a walk along the waterfront; only a couple passers-by came up asking for an autograph, which Vinny did with a showman's flourish. Annie stood by, smiling gently, blushing and offering to take the obligatory photographs when a camera was produced.

'I've had a lovely time tonight,' Annie said. It was a cloudy night and they were standing in front of the office of Haining Cabs.

'I'm really glad,' Vinny said and then shrugged apologetically. 'If it wasn't for that homeless twat screaming 'Oopma Loompa' it would have been perfect.' He smiled a little sadly.

'Hush you,' Annie said and leaned down and kissed him very tenderly on the lips. They broke a minute later, and Vinny reached out and touched her cheek gently.

'Would you like to see me again, Annie?' he asked hopefully, knowing that if he just played this one cool, (she was most definitely into him, and not because of what or who he was) she would be a keeper.

'Yes, I'd like that. Erm, I've got to get back home now though because I've got the seven o'clock shift tomorrow,' she answered, pointing at the taxi office. 'I finish at six tomorrow, would you like to pick me up from outside the hospital?'

'Of course,' Vinny replied, and they kissed again, longer this time, more passionately and Vinny felt himself thinking that he might just find happiness again.

Instead of cutting through the park, like he always did, Vinny decided to take the long way home; a walk that would take a person of normal height about fifteen minutes to do and Vinny— nearly an hour. He stopped off at Himmad's Fish and Chips and bought a small portion of chips and a jumbo sausage only to near-drown them in salt and vinegar. The owner of the shop asked if he could take Vinny's photograph. Vinny said he could if he got the chips for free. The owner said no, outraged by the fact that Vinny was trying to pull a fast one. Vinny smiled his sweetest smile, reached up and grabbed at the wrapped packet, (which the owner thought he had *just* put out of reach) took a fiver out of his pocket, scrunched it up, and flicked it over the counter.

'Keep the change, you miserable, miserable man,' he said, *sotto voce*, and left the shop, blowing on the sausage before he bit into it.

After the meal, he disposed of the empty papers and checked his now working Nokia to see if he had any messages. Annie had left one, reiterating the fact that she had a really lovely time and couldn't wait to see him the following day. He typed his name into the twitter login and checked his mentions—sure enough from @azakhimmad there was: @VinnyDazzle Legend midget fuck is no nice guy. Want fuck everything for free! Fuck you Vinny!

Vinny decided he was in too good a mood to go back to the chip shop and kick off, that he should go home, possibly snort a line or two of cocaine and maybe watch some late night shopping TV or even the live feed of Badgerwatch.

Back home he shrugged off his coat and shoes and put on a woollen jumper and Bart Simpson slippers. The coke was in the bedroom upstairs but he couldn't be arsed to go and get it. Instead he went to the chest of drawers in the lounge and pulled out a book of photographs that contained all of the photos of himself and Mary. He flicked through the pages, taking the odd photo from its cellophane protection and looking at it wistfully; he still missed his wife dreadfully and even though he didn't think he would have had half the fame or support he had if she hadn't died—he would have given it all up just for one more minute with her.

'I think Annie will be good for me,' Vinny said, tears spilling down his cheeks. 'But she'll never replace you, I loved you too much.' He kissed her image.

Maybe it was time to have a couple of lines, after all.

He had left the heating on all day much to his disgust, something that he was usually really good at keeping on top of. He chopped up three fat lines and was pinching his nose and breathing in to try and clear a small blockage of powder that was in his right nostril. The heat came on quickly then, threatening to smother him (he always got this way when on the Charlie) so he walked to the bedroom window and opened it wide. A thick bank of cloud drifted across the sky and confronted Vinny with a full and incredibly bright moon.

He stared at it, blinking, confused at why all of a sudden he couldn't swallow. His throat seemed to have swollen and he raised his hand to massage it. He stopped in horror when he saw that his finely manicured fingernails were elongating and turning a colour more normally seen on a smoker's fingers. He tried to cough; it came out as a choking sound. Black hair appeared on his hands as if by magic, tufts here and there, in no order, randomly curling from his skin. Then a wicked bolt of pain made him scream out, it felt like someone had taken a hold of his jaw, planted their foot on his chest and pulled the bottom half of his face as hard as they could. Vinny fell to his knees with the awfulness of it, as another bolt tore through him, but this time it was his shoulder blades cracking and expanding. His clothing suddenly felt too tight—he tried to take off his jumper but his hands had, in only a few seconds, elongated and fattened too much to respond. The fingernails now looked very much like claws. Claws that could tear through a man's stomach very easily.

Vinny had brief flashes of that deserted road and the thing that had attacked him.

'Oh, fuck me,' he croaked. His voice had changed, deepened, further than the *sotto voce* at the chip shop; it sounded utterly carnal to the point of a growl. His eyes started to bulge, almost pop out. Colours mutated, dulled down, but overall his clarity was improving, everything more defined, more nuanced and precise than he had ever experienced.

The small of his back was the main source of pain now. He felt immense weight pushing down on it and his whole body arched up, as if someone lying on top of him had him in a wrestling hold. He felt his ribcage splay open and his woolly jumper followed, leaving it hanging forlornly around his neck—the sleeves still on his arms. The Bart Simpson slippers tore next, at the seams, his size four feet were now an eleven, coarser black hair covered them, and the claws were a dirty bone white. There was so much agony now that Vinny couldn't focus on one place, his face felt like it was being pushed in on either side of his temple and his nose felt puffy and fat, as if someone had punched him repeatedly. His raspy tongue ran over razor sharp teeth. It was then that cognitive human thought left him and pure, base, animal instinct took over. He barked harshly and the noise filled up the room. He leapt up onto the window ledge and scrambled down the side of the house. Then Vinny was off, chasing a scent, his animal memory taking him to the last place he had smelt blood and pain.

The hospital.

In all, Vinny had stretched out around another two feet in length, and this made him lope across the park much as a gangly lurcher would. Whilst there was no denying that he was now a beast, he clearly wasn't used to being one and it would take time, not long, but it would take time to fully take charge of his limbs. A cat hissed, somewhere off to his left, and Vinny span on the spot and tore after it, thirty seconds later it was dead, its head ripped off, chewed and swallowed in an instant. The guts were ripped out and devoured by his bloody muzzle. He left the bloody pelt behind.

He ran then under the watchful light of the moon. The night was still dark enough for him to be an urban shadow, out of sight to the residents of this upper class, gated estate.

Five minutes later he arrived at the Norwich and Norfolk Hospital and ran around to the back of the building. He stopped, lifted a paw and cocked his head to the sound of a faint cry.

Newborn.

If it was possible for a werewolf to smile, then Vinny was smiling. He licked his chops, the cat's blood tasted metallic, quenching, right. But there were more meals to be had. The were-dwarf started to climb up the side of the building and towards the cries of the maternity wing.

The ringing telephone woke him. He opened his eyes, barely. Light flooded in and made him wail. He felt wet, drenched. Then came the pain. A pain that made Vinny think his body had been utterly broken. He forced himself to open his eyes, his vision was red and wavered as he fought to regain focus. He rolled over onto his back, that cold, sticky wetness again. The previous night came to him, snatches of it at least; of running, of climbing... of eating...

He sat bolt upright; the bed was completely red with blood. He yelped and rolled off in sudden disgust; swinging himself over and landing nimbly. He retreated to the bedroom door, shaking, looking from the bloody marks on the window sill to a bed that looked like the Countess of Bathory had been using it as her private hot tub. The back of the house could not be seen by neighbours, only from the road down below; he was hoping that any blood he may have splashed up the walls would have soaked into the dark porous brick to be rendered invisible to the human eye. An inhuman thought. It was still with him. His mind rambled on—there had been heavy rain towards the end of the night and...

Vinny stopped to look harder at a tiny arm that was poking out from underneath a sodden pillow. His eyes widened and he stopped breathing entirely. It appeared he had brought a late night snack home with him. 'No, no...' he was imploring now as he reached up and pulled the pillow off the bed only to reveal a baby's arm, shoulder and flap of skin from the torso. There was nothing else he could recognise.

The alarm rang. The blood spattered clock read ten am.

Vinny very nearly called the police to hand himself in, the fractured memories of last night now a feature film in full high definition. He'd jumped into the room and ran to the late shift nurse, disembowelling her with one sure flick of his claw. He'd bit into her mouth to forever silence her. The cries of the newborns sounded like a choir of angels...

His mobile started to ring.

As he walked towards it, each step his feet took on the cold wooden floor made him more certain of who was ringing him. He picked up the phone and clicked it live.

'Hello?' he asked, his voice hoarse and raw.

'Vinny, it's me Annie.' She was crying.

'What's wrong Annie, why are you upset?' He left the question hang in the air.

Annie told him what he already knew. She asked him how he hadn't heard, didn't he have his television on? He said that he had slept in, had a few beers when he got back home from their date. She accepted it easily. Why shouldn't she? She said the police were interviewing everyone, the press were crawling all over the place. They were sending non-priority patients home, emergency patients were being sent to three other hospitals in the county and the rest to the large hospital in Ipswich.

'Do you want me to come and meet you after work?' he asked, his voice flat, his eyes staring at the blood on the windowsill.

'Would you?' her voice was full of relief. 'I think we'll be kept here until the police are done with us—they've been asking everyone where they were last night, so the police might come and visit you to confirm my whereabouts. Is it okay if I give them your personal phone number or do you have an agent they need to get in touch with?' Even in the midst of the carnage, Annie was mindful of his "celebrity" status.

'If the police ask, you can give them my phone number, that's not a problem. And as soon as you're done, phone me straight away and I'll come and pick you up. I'm so sorry Annie, it must be awful there.'

'It is,' she seemed to whisper, then the line went dead.

Vinny let the phone drop to the floor, and backed out of the room and went into the shower, trying to wash the burden of his beast away. He knew he would have to shower again after cleaning the room, but for now he had to try and wash away the memories of the night before. In the steam of the shower room, there was someone standing with him, the shadow of his taller, meaner, *killer* self, and it snorted, a low, menacing derision, and to his utter horror Vinny caught himself snorting along with it.

The room had been a nightmare to clean, and now smelt of so much bleach that Vinny's eyes were red raw. He thought he was going to pass out with the fumes, but he battled on, stripping the bloody bed sheets and putting them in the wash before taking them out to hang over the radiator. The bleach had done an okay job, but there were still pink streaks running through them. He began to shred them into thin strips. After that, he slowly cut the strips into hundreds of tiny little squares—it was a pointless exercise but it calmed him. Could he take them to the woods, dig a large hole and let nature take its course? They were cotton after all... There was no time now so he shoved the bag into the farthest corner of the loft, where a fake partition wall was situated, behind which was the boiler. It would have to do.

The baby part was the trickiest thing that Vinny needed to dispose of. He nudged it onto a non-stick baking tray to make carrying it easier and thought he should feel disgusted—by himself, by what he had done, but the initial fright at finding the carnage had been diluted by the fact that he found the situation rather *too* easy to accept. He picked up the tray and padded into the kitchen.

Later in the day, Vinny sat in his now sterile bedroom and mused. He still had time before meeting Annie. His was already a life made hard by being small and now there was this new challenge to overcome; another quirk of fate to triumph over. But he would. The more he thought, the more he felt there was nothing he could *not* conquer. Yes, several nights a month he would become a killing machine, that he knew, but it would be extremely manageable if he just did his research and followed the rules associated with lycanthropy. He would have to make sure that he went out into desolate countryside every time a full moon came around—say in Scotland where he was sure to be fine. The more he thought on it the more he knew it was manageable, the only thing he would have to look out for were errant gamekeepers deer-stalking any time he had to venture up north, but then he was immune to everything bar silver bullets, wasn't he?

He met Annie away from the hospital; with the amount of police and press there it wouldn't do either of them any good if he suddenly turned up. He was in Nutty Nut Cafe, the local Vegan hotspot, and was trying his hardest to drink an apple and flax seed smoothie. His gorge rose with every half-swallow and he was thankful when he saw her scurry around the corner and walk over the road towards the cafe. He got up, smiled briefly at the hippy behind the counter who was nice enough but the smell of the man was beyond disgusting. Vinny didn't think that anyone else was able to smell it though. All of his senses had been heightened, and he had even caught a whiff of Annie's scent when she was more than five minutes away from the cafe, but he just sat there, letting the occasional feather of her musk delight and tease him. But it had to fight its way through hippy stench, and for that the scruff would surely have to meet his fate one moonlight evening in the near future.

'Oh Vinny,' Annie said, bending down slightly to hug him. Her face was buried in the crook of his neck, hot tears dampening his skin. Excitement coursed through his body, his cock twitched in his trousers. He wanted her, her smell was surely going to drive him crazy, his olfactory system was going into over-time; such was the heady intoxication of her musk.

'How's it been?' he managed to say, his voice breaking slightly with need. She appeared not to notice and took him by the hand and walked down the street and towards a pub that Vinny had often passed but had never been into, The Fat Cat.

'As I'm not a part of the Maternity wing, we were just subjected to being taken into a room and asked where we were last night,' Annie said evenly, but not without emotion as they sat in a private booth. Both were drinking alcohol; Vinny was on half a Stella, Annie was on the double vodka and cokes.

'I told them I was with you until we parted for the night,' Annie said quietly, taking Vinny's free hand, the one that wasn't lifting the Stella up to his mouth. 'I told the policeman that it was in the strictest of confidence and that the press wasn't to know as it could possibly detract the papers from being able to help get information out to the public to help trap who killed the children. He heartily agreed with me—he's suggested that once it all dies down that you visit the hospital and donate some money or something, maybe buy them a new CCTV surveillance system as the old one broke down years ago, and you know... with all the cuts...' Annie started to cry in front of him, a terrified young woman utterly bewildered by events beyond her ken. 'What kind of *monster* would do this, Vinny? I overheard some reporters saying that the government are wanting the public to know that it was a rabid fox or something, but people are saying that there are pieces of the babies *missing*...'

He reached forward, placing his hand on hers. And yes, his fingers were still as long. She looked up at him, her eyes glistening, but the look that she gave him was sincere.

'Would you like to take me home Vinny?'

He felt no shame. Only elation.

They took a taxi back, Annie leaning on Vinny's shoulder, he was stroking her hair gently. The taxi driver had tried to talk to them as soon as he'd recognised Vinny, but one withering glance had put paid to that. The driver put the radio on instead, but turned it down low enough so the couple wouldn't be able to hear. But Vinny could, and of course it was all about the carnage in the Norwich and Norfolk. It was plain to hear from the garbled information that was coming through, that the authorities hadn't a clue as to what had happened and probably never would.

The taxi took them to Thorpe St Andrews and to the house that Annie rented on a lovely road called Thunder Lane. Vinny paid the fare and told the driver to keep the change. The driver was so thrilled that he jumped out of the taxi and ran round to the side of the car and opened the door so Annie and Vinny could get out. The driveway was loose gravel and the front garden was a small patch of grass. They came to the red door and Annie got out her keys and unlocked the top lock, then cursed under her breath as the main key stuck in the second. 'It always does this,' she sighed, stepping back as Vinny reached up and pulled the door towards him with some force, and twisted the lock with his other hand. It clicked easily and Vinny pushed the door open for her. She smiled and touched the side of his face gently. It felt electric.

The house was a thirties semi-detached, she wouldn't say any more than that she was free of the mortgage. Annie had simple tastes, a long brown sofa in the living room, with two lighter brown armchairs under the window. An old wooden trunk that served as both shoe storage and occasional table took centre stage in the room. The kitchen led out to one of the most simple yet glorious looking gardens that Vinny had ever had the pleasure to visit. There was a small patio, then a good patch of ground, but beyond that was a small white picket fence that probably housed one of the most cared for vegetable patches in East Anglia.

When they went back indoors Annie made Vinny a cup of tea and they talked about anything and everything except the events. Annie had changed from her uniform and was now wearing a baggy green fisherman's jumper and jeans.

The clock slowly counted the hours and outside the sky changed from blue to fuzzy grey. Vinny looked at his watch and decided that now was the time to order a taxi, go home, close the curtains and sleep like the dead.

'I'd like you to stay,' Annie said, when he made moves to go. 'If you don't mind?'

'Have you *grown*? Is it possible for midgets to suddenly sprout two inches?' Gondola asked as he measured Vinny's inside thigh, shaking his head as he did so. 'I know your measurements off by heart, but you've really thrown me with...' he paused looking at the measuring tape with confusion. 'You have grown! Have you told the papers about this?' He asked looking up at Vinny who was beaming as he stared at his reflection in the mirror.

'It's love,' Vinny said simply, as Gondola brought over some lengths of fabric and held them up to his back to see what would be the best cut and colour.

'And the bride to be is happy to become a part of Britain's hottest celebrity couple?' Gondola smiled as Vinny turned around and picked the blue material which was the one that Gondola would have forced upon Vinny if he had to. His tastes were getting better the taller he grew.

The press took to Vinny's wedding the only way they knew; in a kind hearted but piss-taking manner. **Vinny takes Bride Up the Aisle (if he can reach!)** was *The Sun*'s effort—the *Daily Mail* went for **TV Midget Begs For OK! Rights** which was ludicrous—Hello had sealed the deal when Vinny first told his new agent the news.

The incident at the hospital was still an open investigation, and Vinny had been good at either keeping the curtains firmly closed where there was a full moon, but when the summer nights had started to draw in and the moon was fat no matter that you could still see in front of your face, those were the times he would take trips up to Scotland, always telling Annie that he had to go and do a DJ gig. She never questioned it; and was doing a lot of longer shifts as she had been recently been promoted to ward sister.

The day of the wedding soon came, and the date had been chosen by Vinny so as not to fall on the full moon. The last thing he wanted on either the wedding night or during the honeymoon was to devour his new wife in more than just the carnal sense.

The day went without a hitch, the guests were well behaved, even the celebrities. Before the ceremony had begun, Vinny had a private moment with Mary, his first wife's family, to introduce them to Annie and they gave them their blessing. Annie felt a little weird about that, but Vinny had persuaded her by saying that it was only fair on the family to have.

For the reception afterwards Chico surprised the guests by singing a couple of lovely songs that were not suffused by his 'normal pomp and circumstance' as he liked to call it. Vinny hadn't the heart to tell him that a couple of the guests had thought he was going to throw in his 'famous' catchphrase during the middle eight.

He had found the bothy during his second trip to the Highlands, and it was perfect for his needs. When he had discovered it, Vinny didn't think anyone had used it in at least five years, the newspaper that he had found on the table was testament to that fact.

The preparation that he had put into accepting and living with being a werewolf was nothing short of staggering. All of the information that he had amassed he kept safe on a hidden memory stick and was always sure to delete all pages he visited; the last thing he wanted was Annie to click on a link and wonder why her new husband was looking at pages headed "How to Kill Werewolves in a Modern Day Environment."

He had killed again; Vindaloo, the dog from The Florden Arms was found without its head, several deer which had been culled from the Queen's Estate at Sandringham—but as yet, no humans. While taking care of Vindaloo, he had looked for signs of the other wolf who had turned him, but there was no trace of it, no fresh stool, no carcases that had been left by anything larger than a fox. He didn't think he had killed it when he was attacked, but he would have wounded it.

On those days when he woke up in whatever dedicated "safe house" he had chosen after a night of being his other self, he wondered how many like him were running free within the UK. Vinny thought that the numbers would be quite low, the aim of the werewolf was to feed, not to maim and let go.

The day after Vinny and Annie were married he traded the Trabant for a Freelander, re-sprayed a subdued green; it was perfect for his longer journeys, although the money he spent on fuel sometimes bordered on the absurd.

Vinny also stopped taking the cocaine shortly after the nuptials; it was just going to be too much hassle if he was ever caught by either his new wife or the police—and the cocaine didn't matter anymore; he now experienced one of the greatest highs on the planet. He also decided to let out his place, and after one of the greatest makeovers in history, after persuading his occasional friend, the flamboyant Laurence Llewellyn Bowen, to oversee it for him, he was commanding the highest rent in Norwich, bringing in just a shade over one and a half thousand pounds per month. There were also several television appearances, mainly reality work, but BBC3 were interested in commissioning a documentary about midgets and sex—they were keen to get Annie involved and get her to open up about their relationship, something that Vinny didn't really mind about, there were no problems in *that* department, but so far Annie had refused, she said that what went on in the bedroom remained in the bedroom.

Married life was good. Married life was *great*. Annie had yet to put together Vinny's trips and the full moon but when she did, he didn't think there would be any issues. He felt so on top of his game that he could talk himself out of anything and everything. Their new house (Annie's was currently on the market, the rent from Vinny's was paying the new mortgage) was coming together slowly, they each found the other's tastes to be simple and refrained and Annie adored it when she came home late to find that Vinny had cleaned the house from top to toe and dinner was in the oven.

'We're lost.'

'No, we're not, if we can just find the path that's at the bottom of the hill here, I'm sure it'll take us back onto the road to the hostel.'

'Steve, let's face it, we're lost and you're too idiotic to just admit it. You can't man up and... Steve wait up, I didn't mean what I said, don't leave me behind Steve.'

'You're nothing but an uppity bitch! Whose idea was it to go hill walking in the first place? We could have just had a nice lie in this morning then taken a trip to that little local pub with the fireplace and hung out there all day talking to the local alcoholics and getting merry on the local beer, but oh no, little miss britches wanted to go for a romp in the heather, experience the real Scotland. Well if it wasn't for you and your whining at me when we reached the top of the Glen Pap when the mist came down so quickly, I think I would have had a pretty decent idea of how to get us out and back, but no, we've wandered into some desolate shithole of a valley where it doesn't look like anyone's entered it since the last ice age...'

'You wait till your mother hears about the disgusting way you're treating me, you'd never say anything like this if she were around.'

'You know what Laura? I actually don't care anymore. When we get back, you can phone my mum to come and get you and then you can live a nice little lesbian lifestyle, because you've sure as hell not given me anything on this holiday. I had to beg for a blowjob? What the fuck is with that? I'm on holiday!'

'Don't Steve, there's no need to go into this, it's as clear as it's fucking night that our relationship has crashed and burned.'

'At last, a little spark! And I think it's actually the first time I've heard you swear! About fucking time you grew a pair. Now... what was that noise?

'Steve, it was nothing, stop trying to freak me out more than I am already.'

'No... I mean it, sounded like a low growl, like an angry dog. Wasn't your stomach was it?'

' Steve, what was that? Get me the away from it, RIGHT NOW.'

'I don't know, get the fuck away from me, what is it, oh fuck what is that GROWLING, Laura let go of me, let go, let GO...'

'S T E E E V V V E E E E E E!!! A A A A H H H H H GOD NOOOOOOOOOO...'

The bodies of Steve Evans and Laura Ipswich were found two days later. Laura had filled out the obligatory climber's slip stating where they were going to go and what time they expected to be back. As soon as it was clear that all indications pointed to them being lost, the hostel manager called the police and Mountain Rescue. Within two hours they were searching the Pap of Glencoe—the location that Laura had scribbled down, with no luck. The search area was widened and another search and rescue helicopter was summoned to help the first.

As one of the helicopters flew across Coire Gabhail, the 'Hidden Valley', the spotter located a bright red something, possibly a jacket, lying in amongst a patch of heather. From screengrabs taken from the hostel's CCTV, Steve was last known to be wearing a red waterproof jacket, Laura a blue one.

The two helicopters descended, the sight of them coming into land would have been a filmmaker's wet dream. Other rescuers were coming in through the rough, scrabbly entrance into the valley—it was very rough going for those rescuers on foot, but they were soon told to turn back.

The spotter soon wished he wasn't good at his job.

The remains were scattered. Laura's head was found on top of a rock, eyes, nose, lips and tongue gone. Ragged, thin strips of flesh were gone from her cheeks.

The lower half of Steve was never found.

Vinny drove back home in considerable pain; not from the usual after-effects that he had learned to live and cope with after battling through his 'changing'. While in his other form, just after killing and eating Steve and Laura, his foot had come down hard on a sharp piece of stone, probably flint or slate and had torn a deep six -inch gash into his foot. As wolf, the slice wasn't even noticed, but now, back in human form, the wound was agony and was compounded every time Vinny pressed his foot down on the accelerator. His sock was sodden with blood.

The pain reached its zenith when he got to Scotch Corner; he had to pull over into the hotel car park (the farthest end), for fear he might black out. He crawled into the back of the car, weak with pain, (thankfully the back windows were heavily tinted) and threw up in the footwell, a weak, watery effort. Suddenly a dizzy-ing wave of darkness swept over him and that was it, Vinny dove straight for unconsciousness.

When he came to, an hour later, he crawled back over into the driver's seat and drove the short distance to the Scotch Corner petrol station where he bought some codeine, ibuprofen and a large roll of sticking plaster. Thankfully the station was empty and the old lady who was serving didn't know or care who he was, she even came round to the front of the counter to take his money from him as she was too frail to reach over and take Vinny's cash from him.

Vinny washed down three codeines and an ibuprofen with a can of coke and was glad that the roll of plaster was sufficient to cover his foot. He threw his sodden sock and shoe into the nearest bin. The pain started to ebb away, slowly but surely, and he commenced driving back to Norwich as quickly as possible, thinking he had four hours maximum before the pain returned. He managed to get as far as Cambridge, just over three hours in. The accelerator was slick with blood, his foot kept sliding off it. He pulled over into a lay-by, pulled out his Nokia and brought up the press office phone number of the Cambridge University Hospital and phoned them, hoping beyond hope they'd know who he was.

They did and completely accepted that he was doing a charity 'walking on broken glass' event (the best he could come up with) and told him to make his way to Geriatric Medicine and a porter and someone from the Press team would be there to meet him.

Once he had parked, he hobbled across to the entrance to Geriatric Medicine, trying not to look behind himself, just in case he was leaving bloody smears across the tarmac. He was slightly amazed that he hadn't bled to death on the journey down, but he hadn't been gushing blood, and even though he was small, he still had a good pintage in him.

The porter was there, a nice looking bearded chap, he had a wheelchair waiting. The Press Officer was also there, and even through the intense pain he saw that she was a beauty, and if it wasn't for the fact that he was married to Annie...

He collapsed before he got to the wheelchair.

When he came to he found himself in a private room and someone was working on his foot. He moaned gently, that was enough to get whoever was treating him to stop what they were doing and come tend to him.

'Hello Mr Dazzle, my name is Anton Soya and I shall be your foot doctor for today. I've given you a shot of something to help take the edge off things. You've just come to as I was about to start, but don't worry yourself, you'll be fine. Do we have anyone we can call for you? Friend, relative?'

Vinny looked to one side, his Nokia and wallet were on the

bedside cabinet. He pointed to the phone and Anton walked across and gave it to him. Vinny felt very groggy, trying to lift his arm felt like he was lifting a hundredweight.

Anton went back to Vinny's foot.

'A bit of a nasty injury you have here, I'm just going to tidy up some of the torn flesh.' Anton started to whistle, a not unpleasant trilling. Vinny unlocked the phone, went into contacts and scrolled down the twelve names until he came to Annie's. He pressed her name then held the phone up to his ear, it began to ring.

'It looks like you've sliced through the Adipose tissue and the first layer of muscle, the Abductor hallucis and you've nicked a few blood vessels along the way, nothing major but the reason for your bleeding. I'm going to cauterize the wound with a good solution of silver nitrate then get a second opinion on what operation, if any you'll need.'

'Hello my love,' Annie said, she had picked up on the fifth ring.

Silver. The word cut through the drugged fog of his mind. 'Shit,' he croaked, dropping the phone on the bed and tried to get up as the first bolt of pure, white heat started at his foot and ripped through his body.

Vinny's throat closed up, a high-pitched choking noise escaped his throat. If felt like bubbles of molten lava were growing and bursting in his brain. He went blind, blood vessels in his eyes disintegrating.

'Vinny?' Annie yelled into the phone. 'What's *happening?*' she screamed.

Anton looked on in horror as Vinny's foot seemed to snap in half, then pop back out again. His toenail, that had only an instant before had been chipped, but healthy, was now long, dirty and very, *very* sharp. As another swathe of pain wracked poor Vinny's frame, his foot snickered out and the toe cut Anton's throat from ear to ear, as neat as you please. Anton fell into the table containing his tray of scalpels, solutions, syringes and other medication, scattering them. His blood jetted into the air in front of him and his last moments on earth were spent watching the hellish vision of Vinny being poisoned to death by the one thing utterly lethal to lycanthropes.

And in *his* last moments, Vinny had one fragment of thought, that it was a blessing he had died in human form because the papers would have a field...

Vinny died, and not a trace of his other self was to be found.

Vinny's death, *nay*, Vinny's *murder*, made the papers—but it was dwarfed by what had become the biggest story to ever hit the UK and dominated the papers for months and months to follow.

Azak Himmad, of Himmad's Fish and Chips, Norwich, was being called the 'Beast of Norwich' after a new start at the chip shop, Toby Douglas was sent through to the back of the shop to get a bag of chips from the massive deep freezer next to the back door. Being the nosey type, and looking for something he could steal to take back to his mother, he had a rummage about and pulled out something that looked like a broken baguette. Closer inspection and Toby thought it was a doll's arm. Then he realised that there was a bone sticking out of it.

Mr Himmad wasn't working in the shop on that evening—the police were duly called before Azak was. Lisa, the oft put-upon senior in the shop finally saw a way to utterly fuck him over—she didn't want to give him an inch of running time. The arm was taken away, the shop closed and the newspapers had already been tipped off. While a pleading Azak was arrested at home and then pleading his innocence down at the local police station, tests were being done on the arm and it wasn't long before it was confirmed; the arm belonged to Tabitha Shoebridge, two days old, and a murder victim of the Norwich and Norfolk Massacre.

What made Azak's plight all the more serious were the peeping tom, flasher and three sexual assault charges that he already had to his name. He said he couldn't place his whereabouts on the night of the carnage, he said that after closing up that night he went straight home. He lived alone and couldn't provide an alibi.

His phone was seized, as was his laptop, and on the latter, a trove of rape and one child porn videos were found, enough to nail him as far as the police were concerned. His tweets for that day were examined, and the last one he sent on that day was for the now deceased "celebrity" Vinny Dazzle. It would have been a very minor line of enquiry, only amounting to ask Vinny what had happened between them.

If Vinny had lived he would have been truly amazed at how the internet melted in the days, weeks and months following Azak's arrest. It was an inspired move on his part to get rid of the arm, and he had actually congratulated Azak for foolishly leaving the back door to the fish and chip shop open one evening, making it so simple to break in and hide the arm as deep in the freezer as he could get. Vinny had nearly fallen in, now *that* would have been an exclusive on the front of the papers.

The police in Scotland were scratching their heads as they tried to figure out what had happened to Steve and Laura; they were actually going to put in a request for all the records pertaining to the Norfolk Police enquiry, but once it was established that someone had been arrested for the crime down South and that person had never visited Scotland, they were left to puzzle.

Annie was left with too many unanswered questions, and she knew a cover-up when one was happening—she had been asked once to help cover up a mistake that resulted in the death of a healthy patient a couple of years before. She had gone straight to the ward sister and the person was arrested instantly.

The 'official' line was that Vinny had taken an extreme allergic reaction to the silver nitrate and his heart, larger than normal due to years of excess cocaine abuse had simply given up. This was something that Annie was sure Vinny had never done; there had never been any trace of drug use in all the time they were together; he was a role model. With the death of a patient on his hands, Anton Soya, not the most stable person since the break-up of his marriage, had apparently taken the quick way out, had sliced his throat with the scalpel. Traces of both his blood and Vinny's were found on it.

Annie was never able to find any local charity that was doing a 'walk on broken glass' fundraiser—she wanted the press to release a statement asking the charity in particular to step forward—but Vinny was dead, in the ground and was "of utterly no interest to anyone, anymore," —his ex-agent said harshly to Annie before he hung up on her.

She spent her days watching re-runs of Vinny in several of his television appearances as she got fatter and fatter with their first child. She ate chocolate and patted her belly and wondered with amazement at the amount of kicking the baby did at every full moon.

AUTHOR'S MUMBLES

S hould a minor writer such as myself indulge with the whimsy of saying how his stories came to be? Well, I've always enjoyed reading them in other author's collections, so hopefully you might like to read them in mine.

Aldeburgh: Of all the stories written by M.R. James, 'A Warning to the Curious' is the one I can read over and over without ever becoming tired or jaded by it. The idea of even attempting to write a sequel to it only came about in a phone call I had with Richard Dalby when I asked him if I was to ever write a sequel to a James story, what would be the best one to attempt. He suggested 'The Wailing Well'. I went back and re-read it but couldn't come up with an outline to a possible story that grabbed me. It was then the penny dropped and decided that not only should I write a sequel to 'A Warning' but that it should also feature Montague himself as the main protagonist. Four people need to step to the front here, without whose expertise on the life of Montague Rhodes James, the story would have been much poorer indeed: Reggie Oliver, Roger Clarke, Richard Dalby and Ramsey Campbell. As to the finished story it was originally published in *Terror Tales of East Anglia* by Gray Friar Press.

Mrs Claus and the Immaculate Conception: This story is the fault of Robert Shearman, though he shouldn't be blamed for encouraging it if it's a bad one! It was while at a barbeque at Stephen Jones' lovely house in the summer of 2011 and I was tipsily telling Rob an idea I had about Mrs Claus being 300 years old and pregnant. Rob told me to go ahead and write it, so here it is, even if

Mrs Claus is a little bit older in this version. 'Mrs Claus and the Immaculate Conception' is original to this collection.

Cure: This was specifically written for an anthology that at present has still to see the light of day, so here it is. 'Cure' came about when the rather nasty thought popped into my head of females being able to pass on their cancer to their unborn children with the help of genetically modified drugs. It's not a story I liked writing, and this remains the only story that my wife refuses to read. I don't blame her.

The Tip Run: When I was growing up, the tip was a brilliant place to go to – and as the story says, it wasn't a place that was overly tied down by health and safety laws. The things that you found there were either brilliant or downright disgusting. My father and I often went down on a Saturday morning, then to the golf driving range that was nearby. 'The Tip Run' was originally published in *The Screaming Book of Horror* by Screaming Dreams

Head Soup: This one was written at the same time as 'Final Draft' and was going to appear in *With Deepest Sympathy* as the top and tail stories, but there was quite a bit of it that I wasn't happy with so sat down and re-wrote it. Influenced by my trying to find the ever elusive Pan Horror author Conrad Hill, the character of Peter van Basel is a mixture of Conrad, Basil Copper, Roger F Dunkley and Harry E Turner. 'Head Soup' was originally published in *The Aklonomicon*, by The Aklo Press.

Dead Forest Air: An early short story, written around the 2005 mark. Everything that happened in the story, up till when the party go into the woods while on hallucinogens is true. In reality, we stayed in the pub till closing time, we all went back to the lad's house and continued with the finite art of getting as mashed as possible. 'Dead Forest Air' is original to this collection.

The Rookery: Probably my most autobiographical story in as much that my father was a gamekeeper, and a bloody good one at that. The make of guns, the cabinets in question, the turnip being blown into smithereens, the pheasant rhyme and the story about the wee kid having his guts blasted out are all real things that I have seen, held and heard, and for those with a keen eye may have noticed that the name of Blunderstone Rookery originally featured in Charles Dickens' *David Copperfield*. 'The Rookery' was originally published in *Bite Sized Horror* by Obverse Books.

Prim Suspect: It was only a matter of time before my most excellent of monstrous creations, Mrs Primrose Hildebrand, demanded that she be written about again. That she died at the end of 'With Deepest Sympathy' did pose a slight problem, but the story of Primrose's biggest secret, told before the events of her demise was extremely fun to write about. For fans of Primrose, you may be interested to know that there is at least one more story about her early years to follow at some point in the future. 'Prim Suspect' is original to this collection.

The Jacket: Although it didn't start out this way, 'The Jacket' is the obvious prequel to my other short story of sentient munching, 'The Bag Lady', published in my first collection *With Deepest Sympathy*. The protagonist's name has been changed to tie in with 'TBL' from its original publication in *Alt-Dead*, published by Hersham Horror.

'I Wish': 'The Monkey's Paw' by W.W. Jacobs is a short story that has been often anthologised, adapted for television many times and its themes have even been worked into a full-length novel, the brilliant *Pet Sematary* by Stephen King. This is my take on the story, bringing it bang up to date and setting it in a part of Glasgow that's best not ventured into after dark. 'I Wish' was originally published as a spoken word story in the audiobook '13', edited by Scott Harrison.

George V: This story is for my father-in-law, Bob Pugh. He is a keen stamp collector and it was a bit of a challenge to see if I could pull off a ghost story about stamp collecting, but I think I did okay, though I'm sure that Bob will have his own thoughts on it! 'George V' was originally published in the ebook *Voices from the Past* by H and H Books.

The Were-Dwarf: A story that first bloomed from an event that happened at my father in law's. The conservatory at the back of the house, which we affectionately call the 'dog house' looks onto one of the most beautiful gardens I have ever had the privilege to see. The door to the dog house is nearly all glass, and there would always be this funny looking smudge on the glass every time my wife and I visited. Bob explained that a fox would come right up to the door and look in on him while he was sitting in there doing crosswords or watching the telly. It didn't take much of a leap from me mucking about and saying 'was it a fox, or was it a were-dwarf!' The story was pretty much put on ice until the last night of World Horror Con 2010, when I got very, very drunk (there's that damn alcohol again!) and told Marie O' Regan and Paul Kane that I was attempting to write a story called The Were-Dwarf. This resulted in hoots of laughter. So I had to write it. It is obviously written as an homage to *An American Werewolf in London* and not -because there have been lots of midgets on the telly recently. The nurse, Annie Wilkies, is also a spin on a certain character from

Stephen King's *Misery*, but a lot nicer. 'The Were-Dwarf' is original to this collection.

Also available from
Shadow Publishing

Phantoms of Venice
Selected by David A. Sutton
ISBN 0-9539032-1-4

The Satyr's Head: Tales of Terror
Selected by David A. Sutton
ISBN 978-0-9539032-3-8

The Female of the Species And Other Terror Tales
By Richard Davis
ISBN 978-0-9539032-4-5

Lightning Source UK Ltd.
Milton Keynes UK
UKOW051803100812

197351UK00001B/10/P